When the Guns Fall Silent

They stared at the unexpected find. It was a faded sepia photograph of a football team. In battledress, some grey-green, some khaki-brown, as if posing before a battle. An artful thought crept into Jack's head. When next someone asked him what he'd done in the war, he'd say 'I played football'.

Jack takes his grandson to the First World War Cemeteries in France. The visit brings back all the horrific memories Jack has tried to forget in the years since the war. But the sight of a face from the past helps to remind Jack that in the middle of the carnage and misery, there was one miraculous moment when all the guns fell silent and enmity was forgotten. That Christmas in 1914 was a brief and never-to-be-repeated interval when fighting gave way to football on the frozen ground of No-Man's-Land.

James Riordan was born in Portsmouth and grew up there during the war. After he left school he worked as a postman, a barman, a crate stacker, a railway clerk, and a double bass player before doing his National Service in the RAF, where he learnt Russian. After demobilization he gained degrees from Birmingham, London, and Moscow, then worked as a translator in Moscow. Back in England he lectured at Portsmouth Polytechnic and Birmingham and Bradford universities and from 1989 at Surrey University where he was Professor of Russian Studies. He has written over twenty academic books on Russian social issues and on sport, several collections of folk-tales, and a number of picture books. *Sweet Clarinet*, based on his own wartime recollections, was his first novel for children; it won the 1999 NASEN Award and was shortlisted for the Whitbread Children's Book Award. *When the Guns Fall Silent* is his third novel for Oxford University Press.

To Henry

When the Guns Fall Silent

Best Wishes

James

When the Guns
Fall Silent

James Riordan

OXFORD
UNIVERSITY PRESS

OXFORD
UNIVERSITY PRESS

Great Clarendon Street, Oxford OX2 6DP

Oxford University Press is a department of the University of Oxford.
It furthers the University's objective of excellence in research, scholarship,
and education by publishing worldwide in

Oxford New York

Athens Auckland Bangkok Bogotá Buenos Aires Cape Town
Chennai Dar es Salaam Delhi Florence Hong Kong Istanbul Karachi
Kolkata Kuala Lumpur Madrid Melbourne Mexico City Mumbai
Nairobi Paris São Paulo Shanghai Singapore Taipei Tokyo Toronto Warsaw

and associated companies in Berlin Ibadan

Oxford is a registered trade mark of Oxford University Press
in the UK and in certain other countries

Copyright © James Riordan 2000

The moral rights of the author have been asserted

First published 2000
First published in this edition in 2001

British Library Cataloguing in Publication Data available

ISBN 0 19 275163 8

3 5 7 9 10 8 6 4 2

Typeset by AFS Image Setters Ltd, Glasgow
Printed and bound in Great Britain by
Cox & Wyman Ltd, Reading, Berkshire

To the memory of my grandfather,
Private James 'Kit' Riordan (1881–1962) and
for my grandson, Perry James Riordan

'An amazing spectacle . . . one human episode amid all the atrocities which have stained the memory of the war.'

Sir Arthur Conan Doyle, on the Christmas truce of 1914

'It is perhaps the best and most heartening Christmas story of modern times.'

Malcolm Brown and Shirley Seaton, *Christmas Truce on the Western Front* (Macmillan, London, 1994)

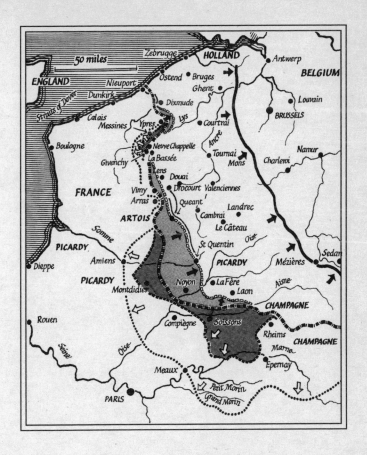

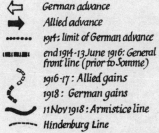

⇦ German advance

⬅ Allied advance

•••••• 1914: limit of German advance

▪▪▪▪ end 1914-13 June 1916: General
front line (prior to Somme)

🔲 1916-17: Allied gains

◾ 1918: German gains

〰 11 Nov 1918: Armistice line

------ Hindenburg Line

1

In Flanders fields the poppies blow
Between the crosses, row on row,
That mark our place; and in the sky
The larks, still bravely singing, fly
Scarce heard amid the guns below.
We are the Dead. Short days ago
We lived, felt dawn, saw sunset glow,
Loved and were loved, and now we lie
In Flanders fields.

from 'In Flanders Fields' by John McCrae

It was so peaceful.

Just the cawing of the crows and the moaning of the wind. Like battlecries mingling with a mother's sighs.

'Up'n at 'em! Up'n at 'em!'

'Hush, my son, sleep, sleep.'

As far as the eye could see stretched row upon row of low headstones: white and clean and even. Like a ghostly army lined up for inspection. Not on a grey parade ground, but on soft green grass, recently mown and dotted with poppies sheltering by the headstones.

It was as if the earth was sown with dragons' teeth. Yet instead of fierce warriors springing forth, the soil had yielded a gentle harvest of stone, lawn, and poppy.

White on green on red.

Truth on Life on Blood.

Why are Flanders poppies such a deep scarlet hue? Are their roots nurtured by Hell's dark streams of blood?

A glossy crow with beady eyes perched on a headstone, like an Angel of Death. Black on white. For all the world resembling that black-edged letter from the King:

The King commands me to assure you
of the true sympathy of His Majesty
and the Queen in your sorrow.

Lombardy poplars stood tall and straight, sentinels of the dead, marking the cemetery boundaries. And dipping and diving in the blue sky above the trees were carefree larks. Today the whole world could hear their song. The guns were silent.

It was so peaceful.

'Grandad, how many Germans did you kill?'

The old man didn't hear. His eyes and ears were in a faraway time that seemed to him like yesterday.

'Grandad, did you stick 'em or shoot their heads off?'

'Grandad!'

'What? Oh, er, sorry, Perry. I was miles away.'

The white-haired old man, pained by memory, looked into the freckled face untouched by war. And his grey eyes wrinkled in a sad smile.

'It was a tidy time ago.'

To a twelve year old that wasn't good enough.

'Did you really kill Germans?'

The last two words crushed the smile.

They opened a door long closed to prying eyes. He'd never spoken about it before. He couldn't.

How would they understand?

Yet now, confronted by dead comrades and a trusting grandson, it was time. It was 1964, fifty years on. He couldn't put it off any more. They all deserved an answer.

It was time.

With a deep sigh that dredged up memories from beneath the silt of time, he said hoarsely, 'Yeah, I s'pose I did.'

'Weren't you scared?'

That was a tough one. How can you explain Fear?

Fear for your own life. Fear for those at home. Fear of being a coward. Fear of letting your mates down. Fear of killing another human being: a son, a brother, a sweetheart . . . a friend.

He was scared all right.

Dead scared. Shivers-down-the-spine, hair-standing-on-end, shit-your-pants scared.

He never told Perry lies. Trust is based on truth. And what greater trust is there than that between grandchild and grandparent?

'I was terrified.'

Perry was disappointed. He'd never seen Grandad scared, never thought of him scared. When they'd started the Great War project at school, he'd boasted of his grandad, the Great War Hero, with ribbons and medals and stuff.

That's how it had all begun.

Yet when he'd asked about the war, all he got was 'It was too long ago.' Grandad wouldn't even come to school to talk about it. He'd written back to Mrs Meneely, 'Sorry, marm, I don't remember.'

What he really meant was, 'I don't *want* to remember.'

Grandad could see he'd let Perry down. In the eyes of his mates, Perry was a 'big-'ed', a 'show-off'. The boy was beginning to wonder whether Grandad really had won the medals. Perhaps he'd bought them second hand?

The old fellow couldn't bear the doubting look. So he had an idea: what if he showed him the old battlefields 'over there'? A quick whizz round France and Belgium. He could take the car on a weekend ferry trip to France and nip round a few war cemeteries.

That way Perry could tell his class what he'd seen for himself.

The old man had never been back. Not in fifty years. Never wanted to. Not even to pay respects to his chum Harry Newell. Nor to his mates Freddie Feltham, Taff Morris . . . and Fritz 'Ginger' Muller.

How *could* they understand?

2

Well, how do you do, young Willy McBride,
Do you mind if I sit here down by your graveside
And rest for a while 'neath the warm summer sun?
I've been walking all day and I'm nearly done.
I see by your gravestone you were only nineteen
When you joined the Great Fallen in 1916.
I hope you died well and I hope you died clean,
Or, young Willy McBride, was it slow and obscene?
from 'The Green Fields of France' by E. Bogle

Side by side, the tall stooping man and straight-backed young boy moved slowly down the grassy aisles, silently and awkwardly, as if in church. The old timer fished his glasses from a Sainsbury bag, rubbed them with his fingers, and put them on to peer at the headstones.

From War Office records he knew roughly where to find his comrades.

'15th Hampshire Regiment. Rows 17–19'

As he read the inscriptions, searching his memory for the dim image of a face to fit a name, icy fingers gripped his heart. He had an eerie feeling that one of those stones would bear *his* name:

PRIVATE JACK LOVELESS
AGED 18
15TH HAMPSHIRE REGIMENT
'HE DIED THAT OTHERS MAY LIVE'

And there was a familiar fresh-faced lad smiling out at

him from the Portland stone, saying, 'No, no, Jack. You lived that *others* may die.'

On every headstone a long-forgotten face appeared, giving him an accusing glare. Only when he reached Harry Newell's grave was the white stone bare. Odd that, for Harry's clear blue eyes and rosy apple cheeks were so fresh in his mind's eye.

A voice in Jack's ear, strongly tinged with Harry's ooo-arrr drawl, made him jump.

'Is this your friend, Grandad? Lumme, he's only seventeen.'

That brought him back to earth.

'Yeah, seventeen, terrible young, ain't it.'

'How did he die?'

'Oh, the usual; blown to bits.'

They both stood still, hands behind their backs, each picturing in his own way a crumpled body flying through the air and falling to pieces on the ground. It was an image they wouldn't dare put into words.

A thin trickle of tears seeped down the channels of the old man's face. Giving his nose a blast on a paper tissue, he dipped his long fingers into the bag again and gently pulled out a rose—the Red Rose of Hampshire.

He'd bought it that day at market.

'*La rose rouge de Picardie. Pour votre amant,*' the old woman had said with a toothless grin.

'*Pour mon camarade,*' Jack had corrected her.

As he bent down to prop the long-stemmed rose against Harry's stone, his arm froze in mid-air. A puzzled frown creased his brow.

'Aye-aye, Harry's had another visit. Recent too. That's bloomin' strange.'

Perry's eyes were drawn to the posy of wild flowers tied with dandelion stems below the stone. His keen eyes spotted something else—beneath the cowslips and

6

clover, poppies and daisies. And he gently teased it out.

The pair of them stared at the unexpected find.

It was a faded sepia photograph of a football team. Not in proper strip. In battledress, some grey-green, some khaki-brown, caps skew-whiff, hobnail boots, and puttees up to their knees—as if posing before a battle.

Yet the folded arms, happy grins, and leather football made it unmistakably a football snap.

'Well, I'll be darned,' said Jack, whistling through his teeth.

He took the photo from Perry and brought it close to his eyes. Slowly, a smile of recognition spread across his face; and an artful thought crept into his head. When next someone asked him what he'd done in the war, he'd say, 'I played football.'

That'd flummox them.

Perry was fascinated by the happy long-ago figures facing death. Who were they?

Grandad responded to the unasked question.

A gnarled forefinger poked at a sweaty player at the back, sleeves rolled up, braces holding up trousers. Time couldn't disguise the lopsided toothy grin.

'Is that *you*?' Perry burst out before Grandad could speak.

'Well, even *I* was young once,' said Grandad, doing his best to imitate the toothy grin. 'That's Harry, top right . . . and Erich, our goalie, next to Fritz our captain.'

'What regiment are those last two? They're wearing a different uniform.'

'Oh, they're German. Same as Hans here and . . . wassisname? Sergeant Schumacher—never did get to know his first name. Well, I'll be jiggered, fancy that. Seems like only yesterday . . . '

Perry was puzzled.

7

'But weren't you *fighting* Germans? They were the enemy . . .'

For several moments only the cawing of crows filled the air. Then Grandad said simply, 'It was Christmas.'

As if that explained everything.

'Anyway,' he said, returning to the present, 'who the hell put it here? And damn recent by the look on them flowers.'

There was nobody in sight.

'I did see a couple of people in that other place,' offered Perry.

Next to the British cemetery, hidden by poplars and a hawthorn hedge, was another field of the Fallen. They'd noticed rows of black crosses as they drove past.

'Let's take a look-see,' said Grandad. 'Spooky, eh?'

Replacing the football snap, he stretched his creaking back and marched off on stiff legs, trying to keep up with the boy's eager strides.

'Hold on, matey,' he called. 'Let's take a short-cut through the hedge. That should bring us out into the other graveyard.'

Perry slammed on the brakes and veered right, waiting for the rickety old pins to catch him up. Together they made for the hawthorn hedge, squeezed through a gap and emerged into another well-kept field. The only difference was the row upon row of *black* crosses.

Although from afar it looked neat and tidy, they could now see that wind and rain had taken their toll. Red rust had eaten into the black iron, like earthworms burrowing into the dark soil.

'This must be the German war dead,' said Grandad in hushed tones.

Sure enough, what names they could make out were foreign-sounding: Walter Krüger, Manfred Müller, Friedrich Kübart . . .

8

What they shared with the Hampshire lads was their age: seventeen, twenty, sixteen . . .

'Fancy dying at sixteen,' said Perry. ''S not right. I bet *we* didn't send young boys to war.'

'Do you know how old the youngest British soldier to die was?'

'Sixteen? Seventeen?'

'Private John Condon died in May 1915 at the age of . . . fourteen. Poor little bleeder. 'S a fact.'

For a moment, Perry was silent. Then he muttered, 'War's crap.'

'Yeah, well . . . it did for ten million altogether—a whole generation of youngsters; the war to end all wars. What a joke.'

They shielded their eyes from the sun, scanning the graveyard for a sign of life. The ancient eyes saw only countless black crosses standing erect in the soil like charred bones.

But the youthful eyes spotted a black-coated figure in the far corner; it reminded him of Grandad, wearing a heavy overcoat on a hot summer's day.

'Over there, Grandad. Come on.'

But the old veteran was having second thoughts.

'Hold hard, matey. What'll we say? Hiya, Fritz. Nice day for a war . . .'

But Perry was off, out of earshot, striding towards the black figure. He'd never met a real live German, though he'd seen German footballers on telly. Pretty good too; not so tricky, mind, as French or Italian.

As he came closer he made out two figures. One was frail and bent, leaning on a stick, white hair flapping under a grey leather cap. The other was a young girl, fair-haired, in a blue and white polka-dot dress.

He stopped to relay the news to Old Puffing Billy, limping along two grave-rows back.

'There's two of them, Grandad. Some old geezer and a blonde girl, laying flowers on a grave.'

This time he waited for the old man to catch up before walking on. By the time they reached the top of the last row, the two figures were sitting on the grass. They seemed to be talking to the grave.

'Saying a prayer, by the looks of it,' mumbled Grandad. 'Let's not disturb them. Come away.'

They were about to turn back when the oddest of sounds came floating over the field. It was someone singing 'God Save the Queen'!

3

And two things have altered not
Since first the world began—
The beauty of the wild green earth
And the bravery of man.

from 'The Bravery of Man'
by T. P. Cameron-Wilson

Grandad stood up straight, shoulders back, chest out, as if on parade again, responding to some long-forgotten command. While the anthem was sung, his head was bowed in respect for the dead, friend and foe alike.

As the last words rang out across the field, he quickly turned about, keen to sneak off before being spotted.

But the boy had other ideas. He was excited at the chance of meeting his first Germans—so's he could tell his class what they looked like. Not only that. He could try out the few words he'd learned in the German lesson. The first word that came to mind was German for 'father', the one the class had giggled over: *Vater*—except the red-faced teacher had pronounced it 'Farter'.

He smiled, desperately trying to knock together a few words of greeting.

As the two dithered at the end of the row, the blonde head suddenly turned their way; the girl was putting something back into her rucksack. Seeing the strangers, she bent her head towards the man and muttered something they couldn't catch.

'We can't go now,' said Perry; 'they'll think we're body snatchers.'

'Don't be daft,' said Grandad. 'Nosy Parkers more likely.'

Just then the old fellow glanced round, his head slightly tilted, gazing above their heads at the wheeling skylarks. He said something to the girl, evidently a question. For she kept darting glances their way, turning back and whispering in his ear.

Finally, the girl pushed herself up, smoothed down her frock and walked unsurely towards them. Man and boy watched uneasily as she approached over the carpet of grass. When she came within ten paces, she stopped and said abruptly, like someone on sentry duty:

'*Guten Tag. Sind Sie Engländer?*'

It sounded like 'Halt! Who goes there?'

She looked slightly older than Perry, perhaps thirteen or fourteen, though she could have been his sister judging by the sprinkling of freckles on nose and brow.

Since they clearly did not understand, she bit her lip and tried again, this time in a low faltering voice:

'Are you Englanders?'

Their faces relaxed and the old man hastily replied, 'Yes, yes, young lady. We came over for a couple of days, you know, same as you by the looks of it, eh?'

'*Langsam, langsam,*' she said with a nervous giggle at the gush of words. She'd never heard English spoken by Englishmen before; they obviously didn't speak it properly, not like her teacher.

The old soldier tried again, even faster than before, but louder, as if by shouting he could make her understand.

'What'ya singin' our national anthem for in a Jerry cemetery? You gave us a bleedin' shock.'

She appealed to the boy, 'More slow.'

Perry understood.

'This . . . is . . . my . . . grandad. He was a . . . soldier.'

She followed that, smiled and nodded, then pointed towards the bent figure by the graveside.

'*Grossvater*. Old soldier also.'

'Grandad asks, Why do you sing "God Save the Queen"?'

To accompany his words, Perry hummed the tune: 'Da-da-da, da, da-da . . .'

She gave a laugh, covering her mouth with her hand; then she took up the tune, but with German words: '"*Heil Dir im Siegeskranz . . .*" It was our hymn also . . . when *Grossvater* was a soldier.'

The English grandfather suddenly elbowed in, his face lit up by memory.

'Oh yeah, I remember now. The Jerries used to sing it in their trenches; we used to think they were singing our anthem, cheeky beggars. Evidently, our royal lot brought it over from Germany. They liked the tune so much, they gave it English words and made us all sing it.'

The girl shrugged her shoulders and held out a hand. 'My name is Gretel—as in Grimms' fairy tale.'

She gave a shy smile.

Taking her warm hand, the boy said, 'I'm Perry. This is Grandad.'

Grandad shook her hand stiffly.

'Come,' she said softly. 'Come, meet *Grossvater*.'

She turned and led the way to the corner grave, with Perry close behind and Grandad bringing up the rear.

The old German's face was turned eagerly towards the approaching footsteps. As they came closer, Perry glanced from the silver stick to the sightless upturned eyes, and whispered in Grandad's ear, 'He's blind.'

Grandad said nothing. His face was taut and pale. There was something familiar about the squatting figure that took him back fifty years. No, no, it couldn't be. The day had been so full of ghosts . . .

13

'How do you do,' he said awkwardly, bending down to shake the German's outstretched hand. 'Nice day, isn't it?'

The German's eye muscles twitched as if trying to give sight to blank eyes. His grip tightened on the strong hand.

'Jack?' he said.

'Erich!'

4

Kaiser Bill went up the hill
To play a game of cricket,
The ball went up his trouser leg
And hit his middle wicket.
                    Children's chant

Portsmouth 4 August 1914

It was George Street's last day before the summer break. The whole school was packed like sardines into the hall that morning, girls and boys sitting cross-legged on the wooden floor, teachers lined up on the platform.

Although the mood was perky, you could have heard a pin drop as the doors flew open: and in swept the Headmaster, Mr Cleal—a short, stocky, bald-headed man with a bristling ginger moustache and tufts of hair poking out of his nose and ears.

He briskly climbed the creaking steps and strode to the lectern, glaring down at the squatters. Impatiently, he waited for coughs and wheezes to die down, shifting his glasses up and down on his nose, and twitching his shoulders—sure signs of trouble brewing. When he gripped the lectern sides hard, his knuckles stood out like white marbles on the red hairy hands.

A hush hung over the hall. The lull before the storm.

Old Gingernob was about to give his end-of-term sermon; its message had to last all summer long.

What was it this time?

Boys had been caught smoking Woodbines in the lavs again? 'Disss . . . gusting!'

The football team was letting the school down? 'Disss . . . graceful!'

Heads were to be searched and oiled for nits? 'Disss . . . tasteful!'

Maybe it was more serious today since there'd been no warm-up acts: no Bible readings, no hymn-singing, no school notices.

'School!'

The word exploded like a gunshot.

It got instant attention; even Daisie Brown stopped scratching her itchy bum.

'It is my duty to inform you [long pause] . . . '

The growl was low and menacing.

Had some bigwig died? A school governor they'd never heard of?

' . . . WE ARE AT WAR!'

Oh no, not again! We were *always* at war, putting out fires all over our 'Great Empire', the empire on which the sun never set, the greatest empire that ever was . . . tra-la-la, fol-de-rol . . .

Who was it now? Not those boring Boers again? Zulus? Russkies? Ungrateful Hindus?

> 'Ginger, you're barmy,
> Went to join the army,
> Got knocked out
> With a bottle of stout,
> Ginger, you're barmy.'

But Gingernob had a surprise up his sleeve.

'The Kaiser's army has invaded poor gallant Belgium. It is *our* duty to stick up for the weaker nations. Today Belgium and France, tomorrow England!'

This was serious.

Omdurman, Rorke's Drift, Ladysmith, Balaclava—they were all far away, places only to be found in school atlases. But Belgium and France were just across the English Channel. Some reckoned you could see France from Southsea beach on a clear day.

Now, why would Kaiser Bill invade England? Wasn't he one of us? A Saxon, Queen Victoria's grandson, King George's cousin or something? His mum was English—couldn't she have a word in his ear?

Mr Cleal was about to educate them.

'You will know that, on 28th June, the Austrian Archduke Franz Ferdinand and his good lady were shot by Serbians . . . Not cricket!

'On 23rd July, Austria declared war on little Serbia. Foul play!

'Germany joined Austria. Our friends the Russians stuck up for Serbia, and France sided with Russia.

'Yesterday, the third of August, Germany invaded Belgium. Today, we declared war on Germany. Someone must teach them fair play, eh school?'

His eager eyes appealed to the open-mouthed children before him.

'Well, they've picked a nice day for it,' whispered Floss to her twin sister Doss in the back row.

'Our last day at school and all,' said Doss. 'We're going to miss old Ginger's war bulletins.'

'Shame!'

They both tittered.

Mr Cleal was a patriot. In his morning addresses, he never failed to mention any special battle anniversary; sometimes he made the entire school stand to attention for a full minute. Once Lucy Griffiths wet her knickers through having to stand still so long—her little pool marked the glorious charge of the Light Brigade.

Now, he was off, pounding the wicked Germans, the hideous Hun, the blooming Boche, a nation of criminals, cockroaches to be stamped upon. What made him furious was that he'd have to scrap his walking holiday in the Bavarian Alps.

Poor Mr Dwerryhouse, the Maths master, shuffled awkwardly behind the Head, his face red with shame at being part of the German race (his mother came from Berlin).

After an hour of reminding the school of England's splendid past, of Germany's nastiness, of those former pupils and masters who'd brought glory to the school by laying down their lives for England, Mr Cleal had worked himself up into a real tiswas. He looked as if he'd go off like a half-filled balloon, whizzing up to the ceiling with a rude noise.

However, to everyone's surprise, he suddenly fell silent and stood to attention. Up from his boots came a strange gurgle; and out of his throat issued a tuneless noise:

'God Save our Gracious King,
Long Live our Noble King,
God Save our King . . . '

Caught on the hop, Mrs Scuddymore at the piano and all the platform teachers tried desperately to catch up, though they were always a word or two behind, like hollow echoes in a tunnel.

Without any bidding, the whole assembly uncertainly got to its feet and joined in as best it could, dumbly mouthing words it couldn't remember.

It was one of the most stirring moments in the school's history.

'Isn't our anthem German?' Mr Dwerryhouse drily remarked to the art teacher Mr Buist. Mr Buist sang even louder.

The Head had one last surprise up his sleeve.

After the national anthem, he said briefly, 'That is all. You may go home. Goodbye, school.'

He was not to know how final that farewell was to be.

5

We are Fred Karno's army,
  The ragtime infantry,
We cannot fight, we cannot shoot
  What bleeding use are we?
And when we get to Berlin
  The Kaiser he will say
Hoch! Hoch! Mein Gott!
  Vot a bloody rotten lot,
Vot a bloody rotten lot are they!
                    Popular song

The war news had upset school routine. Old Gingernob should be giving school-leavers a rousing send off. The twelve year olds would be entering the big wide world with his words ringing in their ears.

'Now then, school. Some of you lads are about to set foot on the first rung of life's ladder. What a proud moment, passing from boyhood to manhood, the future fathers of our nation.

'Some of you have been lucky enough to win an apprenticeship in His Majesty's Dockyard. You will learn the trade of shipwright, coppersmith, foundryman, riveter. You'll be taking home your first wage.

'On this, your last day at school, I say: go forth as boys. Return as men.'

He always made it sound as thrilling an adventure as discovering the South Pole, scaling Everest, playing for England. Not at all the dirty, sweaty, boring, seven-to-five, six-days-a-week grind their fathers grumbled about.

Not a word about the girls, future mothers of the nation. No noble job of work for them. Their path was girlhood to motherhood, their workplace was the home: scrubbing, cooking, washing, knitting, bringing up their ration of ten or more kids.

It wasn't worth a mention. It was taken for granted.

What now though? War! War could change all that. It offered *hope*—for boys and girls alike.

For boys, it shone a light down the dark tunnel of toil. It offered adventure, in foreign parts, a chance to break life's unending cycle of poverty and boredom.

Of course, no George Street boy dreamed of becoming an officer. Good Heavens, no! But through luck or guts they might rise above the throng, swap overalls for smart uniforms, gain a stripe, a ribbon, even a medal. Girls would admire them. Mothers would be proud.

No one gave a thought to dying.

For girls, too, war offered a glimmer of hope of a better life, a way out of drudgery. When the menfolk marched away, someone would have to turn the lathes, keep accounts, make bombs and shells, drive the trams and buses. Had they thought of that?

Now, however, war could not be further from the minds of the boys and girls who streamed out, whooping and hollering, from George Street Elementary School.

The sun was shining in a clear blue sky.

The day was young.

Summer holidays stretched ahead.

After picking up their little brother and two sisters, Floss and Doss shepherded them home, past the Mermaid pub, the graveyard, St Winifred's Church, down the terraced, bloodred-brick streets, to No. 39 George Street.

Each was bursting to tell Mum the news.

It was Elsie, the youngest of the crew, who squeezed in the front door first.

21

Mum was in the backyard, putting wet washing through the mangle.

Rushing through the passage and out the back door, Elsie squawked, all out of breath, 'Mum, we're going to have a war.'

Mother had heard. She wasn't at all pleased. The holidays were bad enough, what with nine kids on her hands for six weeks.

'Don't bawl,' she said, putting a wet finger to her thin lips, 'or you'll wake the twins. Now you're home, stick Reggie's dummy back in his mouth and rock the pram.'

She nodded towards Reggie, her most recent arrival; there was yet another 'cooking in the oven'.

'Mum, we're going out to play,' said Doss. 'Need anything down the shop?'

She gave a weary shake of the head, picked up the zinc washboard and began scrubbing brown-stained knickers to the twin chorus of wails from indoors.

'God, I wish I could go to war,' she sighed.

Her thoughts turned to her hubby. If Bert got called up, what then? How would she cope with nine hungry brats and another on the way? Of course, her mum would muck in; she always did despite her aches and pains. But even so . . .

Without Bert's wages, and the bits and pieces from their allotment, goodness knows how she'd make ends meet.

Couldn't they put it off for a few years?

By then her eldest, Jack, would've left home, probably got himself married; Doss and Floss would be fourteen, old enough to help out and fend for themselves . . .

If politicians had her life they wouldn't have time for war.

Later that day, on his way home from work at Campion's bakery, Jack called at his mate Harry's house.

22

His mum was standing in the doorway, propping her youngest nipper on one hip and giving Harry a tongue lashing for getting home from the dockyard so early.

'Get him out of my hair, Jackie,' she shouted. 'And don't you come back till teatime—or I'll belt you one.'

Jack and Harry dribbled the hard rubber ball along the pavement, in and out of the gas lampposts, the dog turds, and parked bikes.

'Well, what d'ya reckon to it?' asked Harry.

'Wha'? Saturday's match?'

'No, you daft ha'p'orth, this war lark!'

'Not the foggiest. They'll likely change their minds by teatime.'

Both lads were promising footballers; they'd had trials for Portsmouth and played the odd match for the youth team. Jack was a rangy goalkeeper, tall for his age, as skinny as a beanpole. Harry was small and nuggety, a nippy right winger.

They were coming up for seventeen next month, when they were hoping to make Portsmouth Reserves. Who knows? That could be the first step to fame and fortune. Maybe in time they could chuck up their jobs and become full-time pros?

'One thing I'll say for war,' said Jack, scuffing the ball against a forecourt wall, 'it might give a few first-team players their call-up papers.'

'So Pompey'll need a speedy winger.'

'And a lanky goalie.'

'Roll on war.'

6

Jack was right.

Within a couple of weeks, six first-team players had joined the colours. No one forced them. No one said 'Show an example to other youngsters'. They just upped and went, queued for hours in the rain down at Lake Road Recruiting Office.

Perhaps Lord Kitchener's handlebar moustache had something to do with it. It followed you everywhere. A whopping great poster plastered on street corners, pillar boxes, and lampposts.

There was old Kitchener glaring at you, pointing at YOU, those snake eyes looking straight down the gun-barrel arm.

'Your Country Needs YOU'

You could almost imagine him leaping out of the poster, grabbing you by the scruff of the neck and bellowing in your face.

'You, You, You! That's right, lad, I mean YOU!'

In the daytime, Jack and his mates would poke fun at the silly old buffer, jabbing their fingers at little girls, twirling an imaginary moustache and snarling, 'Your country needs YOU!'

The poor kids would flee in terror as the older boys marched away in a gang, laughing their heads off and singing:

'My old man's a dustman,
He fought against the Huns,

He killed ten thousand Germans
With only a couple of bombs.
One lay here, one lay there, one lay round the corner
And one poor soul with a bullet up his 'ole
Was crying out for water.'

Of a night time in bed, however, the boys weren't so
bold. More than one had nightmares. A giant moustache
would be smothering them, stuffing their mouths full,
choking the living daylights out of them. A gloved hand
would be at their necks and an iron-hard finger would
be hammering on their heads until their eyes popped
out.

'We need YOU! We need YOU!'

It was like the rat-tat-tat, rat-tat-tat of machine-gun
fire.

Jack's dad reckoned it was all a cunning plot, got up
by some secret government office, to hypnotize people into
joining the army.

'It's always the nobs who're keen on war,' said Dad.
'They live on war, and live in peace on war. Workers see
war as a disaster right from the start; they're the ones who
have to do all the dirty work and stop the bullets.'

Dad shaved off his moustache in protest.

Despite Dad, a war fever was sweeping through the
streets like the Black Death. All of a sudden, newspapers
discovered the evils of the foe, the true face of the enemy
they were up against.

The innocent English, being cut off by sea all round
their little island, hadn't witnessed the beastly crimes of
the horrible Hun. How could they know that Germans
living in England, who had always pretended to be so
nice—and who cunningly looked like us—were plotting
the most dastardly crimes?

With every passing day the papers informed readers of

new plots and crimes; and these were chewed over in home and pub each night.

Eyewitness Account of Hun Horrors

Lady Askwith-Smythe yesterday visited Belgian refugees in a Paris hospital. During her visit she overheard a Belgian girl ask her mother to blow her nose for her. 'A big girl like you, who can't even use her own handkerchief!' snorted the English lady.

The child said nothing, but her mother replied, 'Madame, she has no arms,' and burst into tears.

It turns out that German soldiers chop off the arms of Belgian children to stop them taking up weapons against them. (*Sunday Chronicle*)

The Times had proof. It showed pictures of Germans slicing off children's hands. One captured German was reported to have the fingers of seventeen children in his pocket!

If *The Times* said so, it must be true.

Other papers ran stories of babies nailed to walls on Belgian squares, of a German soldier ripping an infant from its mother's arms, tossing it in the air and catching it on his bayonet.

They claimed to be Christian men. Yet they strung up Belgian priests as clappers in church bells ('Must have made a ghastly BONG!' said Harry).

The trouble with the British was that they were too soft, too trusting. They hadn't realized that Germans had been planted in their midst long before the war by the German High Command—as spies and saboteurs.

Who would have thought that meek and mild Mr Grubbel, who ran the barber's shop down the road, was secretly slitting throats and dumping the dead bodies in his cellar, like Sweeney Todd?

No one suspected that Otto the greengrocer on the High Street was poisoning his sprouts and swedes to destroy the British race. So that's why old Ma Figgins had got the trots and died in agony with the gip!

Who could have known that the smart-suited, bowler-hatted gent, who sang in the church choir and owned a soap factory, was all the while melting down dead bodies to make oil and soap (that's why it was red!) to send back to Germany?

Now that the truth was out, exposed by our trusty newspapers, the British could fight back. Even if they couldn't make it across the sea to Belgium, they would clobber nasty foreigners living in England.

Of a lunchtime and after church on Sundays, well-bred gents in natty suits would march down the street with walking sticks over their shoulders. They were heading for German 'establishments' to teach the fiends a lesson.

And when the pubs turned out at night, mobs of bold brave lads hit back for England in the dark, smashing windows, looting shops, beating up 'aliens', as Germans were now called.

For their own safety (as well as to stop them spying and murdering), the police had to put these enemy aliens in prison.

The government did its best to winkle the Hun out of every nook and cranny of English life. Notices appeared in newspapers.

'The Government has banned the playing of all "alien" music.'

So bride and groom had to trip down the aisle without Mendelssohn's 'Wedding March'! As for his 'Funeral March', the dead had to be laid to rest without its sombre strains echoing in their ears. Some played 'Rule Britannia' instead.

'It is henceforth an offence to call German shepherd dogs "German shepherd dogs". They are to be known as "Alsatians".'

That was one in the eye for Jerry! He wouldn't fancy the new bulldog spirit one little bit.

On the quiet, the king was thinking of changing his name: Saxe-Coburg-Gotha really gave the game away. He would keep the 'George', but call himself 'Windsor' after his castle. Cunning ruse that; kings usually called castles after themselves . . .

A few other Germans living in England tried the same trick. But since they owned no castles, they had to stick to their nasty German-sounding names.

'Serves 'em right for being German,' the Dog and Duck landlord, Willy Forster, remarked.

And he removed German sausages from the menu in his eating parlour; he called them boiled bangers instead.

7

To everything there is a season, and a time to every
purpose under the heaven,
A time to be born, and a time to die; a time to plant,
and a time to pluck up that which is planted;
A time to kill, and a time to heal; a time to break
down, and a time to build up;
A time to weep, and a time to laugh; a time to
mourn, and a time to dance . . .
A time to love, and a time to hate; a time of war, and
a time of peace.

Ecclesiastes 3: 1–8

When Jack and Harry turned up for football after work on Monday evening, Gordon Neave the kitman called them over.

'The boss wants you two, in his office. Now!'

This was it. The call up. Big time. Pompey Reserves?

They were right . . . and they were wrong.

After knocking politely on the office door, at the command 'Enter!' they shuffled in and stood expectantly before the manager's desk. They'd never made it to the holy of holies before.

Jock Brown was a thick-set fellow with iron-grey hair slicked down with water; he was gazing absent-mindedly through the dirty window pane, down on to the lush green pitch. For a few moments he ignored the two youngsters, lost in his own troubled thoughts: his son Ewan had been one of the first to enlist and was somewhere 'over there' in the trenches.

Slowly, he looked them up and down, as if buying heifers at market.

In a broad Glaswegian accent that England had done nothing to tame, he said, 'Are y'up ta fitball, you'se twa?'

'Yes, sir,' they replied in chorus.

'Aye, well, I didna expect a nay. Ya're in ma team for Saturday. Dinna let me doon.'

They were chuffed. To make the Reserves was brilliant, one step short of glory.

'We'll not let you down, Mr Brown,' said Jack eagerly.

'Thank you, sir,' added Harry. 'I know we're good enough for the Reserves.'

'It's nae the Reserves I'm talking aboot,' the manager growled, half to himself. 'It's the first team. Aye, I widna pick ya, but I'm doon to ma wee laddies, what wi' the war an' that.'

They stared at each other, hardly able to believe their ears.

They were playing for Pompey! Pulling on the famous royal blue jersey and white shorts, sporting the city's star and crescent badge.

Jock Brown's stern voice broke into their thoughts.

'Now heed this. It's the Club's job to take minds off the war, keep spirits up. It's a big responsibility. Are y'up ta it?'

'We'll do our best, sir,' said Harry.

'England expects every man to do his duty,' said Jack with a mock salute. It was one of Ginger Cleal's favourite sayings.

'Aye, an' Scotland tae,' growled the manager.

His mind was evidently on other things, for he returned to staring at the pitch. It was as if he was looking down upon a battlefield, seeing the mangled bodies of *his* boys, *his* young players, the waste of so much talent, the war heroes who'd never live to be football heroes . . .

The new Pompey stars turned to go. But as they were halfway through the door, he called them back.

'Ma players are part of the war effort,' he suddenly said. 'I'll ha' no shirkers here. You'se'll report to the drill hall tomorrow at seven sharp.'

Their faces fell.

'Aye, well,' he grumbled, 'I've barely a body left to train ye. The drill sergeant'll keep ye on yer toes. Dinna forget: seven sharp!'

One nil up or one nil down?

'I guess it's worth a bit of drill for Pompey's sake,' said Jack as they clattered down the tunnel and out on to the pitch.

'You're right, Jack, this war's got its good points. Who'd have thought we'd be playing for Pompey so soon? If this war carries on we could find ourselves playing for England.'

'Fighting for England, more like,' said Jack.

They flung themselves into training as never before. This was serious stuff. They were to make their debut against Southampton in the season's opening match. Of all teams they had to beat their south coast rivals; they couldn't let the fans down.

That evening, muscles aching, they limped down to the drill hall at five minutes to seven. The entire football squad had been detailed to report, so they weren't short of friendly faces. But there was another familiar figure in the hall—a stocky, bald-headed, middle-aged man with a ginger moustache. Mr Cleal.

Gone the musty old suit, winged collar, and black tie. Gone the thin cane—his 'whacker'—he always carried about as a sign of authority. He was dressed smartly in shiny boots, brown serge trousers, a field jacket criss-crossed by a glossy leather belt, and a neat grey shirt and tie. In place of the cane he was holding a short stick.

31

On seeing the former George Street boys, his eyes shone through his glasses and he exclaimed heartily, 'Ah, Loveless and Newell, we meet again.'

'Hello, Mr Cleal,' said Jack with an uncertain smile.

Mr Cleal's face quickly changed and his voice hardened.

'You cadets will address me as Captain Cleal. There's a war on in case you hadn't heard. It's our job in the Reserve to lick you recruits into shape. Now, go and get kitted out and be back here promptly at nineteen-thirty hours. Move!'

Cadets?

Reserve?

Recruits?

They were footballers. No one had said anything about them being recruits. They were too young for the army, thank God!

'Well, what a turn-up for the book,' said Jack. '*Captain* Cleal, eh? Put a uniform on him and he's a right little Napoleon!'

'I don't like the sound of this,' was all Harry said.

But Captain 'Ginger' Cleal wasn't the only unwelcome surprise. When they were lining up in their mildewy fatigues, they heard a familiar voice that made them jump.

'Hanging Judge' Jeffries, their old PT teacher.

Now Colour-Sergeant Jeffries.

As smart as ever, in trousers and shirt with razor sharp creases—and three stripes on both arms—he strutted before the boy soldiers, thumping the palm of one hand with a cricket stump.

'Right, you 'orrible little men,' he snarled. 'It's my job to turn you snivelling rabble into disciplined soldiers. You miserable lot are England's Reserve, the country's secret weapon.'

With a smirk towards his headmaster, he bawled, 'Heaven help us if England has to rely on you!'

His hollering suddenly quietened to a snake's hiss.

'Break you in I will!'

For the next hour and a half, 'Judge' Jeffries had the boys marching up and down, drilling with dummy rifles, doing press-ups, sit-ups, running on the spot, rope climbing, and hanging from wall bars.

At the finish, they were certainly fit—fit to drop. They could hardly drag themselves home.

'Much more of this and we'll be knackered out for Saturday,' said Jack with a groan.

'We've *got* to give Friday a miss,' said Harry. 'It's the night before the game.'

'It's either the First Team or the Reserve,' quipped Jack. 'We can't be in both at the same time. Which comes first: football or war?'

It was no contest.

'Mutiny in the ranks already!' said Harry with a weary smile.

8

The first match of the season was always a big event in the city. But this was special, a 'Derby' game against local rivals. Pompey v. Saints. Despite the war, a sizeable crowd packed into Fratton Park, swelled by the many new sailors in port.

Jack's dad stood behind the Fratton goal with the girls Doss and Floss. Harry's mum wouldn't let his dad skip overtime work; but his two uncles had come along to cheer on their nephew.

It was a warm sunny day as the two sides took the field—Blues to Fratton, Reds to Milton end. Both teams fielded players unfamiliar to the fans: a bloke had walked round the running track before the game holding up a blackboard with the teams chalked on it.

Pompey were the unluckier, with so many former stars in the Navy. Still, whoever wore royal blue, or red and white stripes, was Us or Them, and got roundly cheered or booed.

'Don't forget the manager's words,' said the Pompey captain as they lined up. 'This is a big game. Don't let Portsmouth down.'

As the Pompey Chimes rang out from the terraces, the game kicked off. With their strength and experience, Saints were 2–0 up by half-time, and the crowd was silent. Now and again, fans behind Jack's goal vented their frustration on him.

'Butterfingers! You should have saved both goals.'

'Who *is* that clown in goal anyway?' asked someone loudly.

The second half went much like the first, and the fans started to show their anger. No longer did they get behind the team, urging them on. Now they got on to their backs, telling the players what they thought of their efforts.

'You clumsy oaf,' shouted a fan at Jack. 'You're too slow to catch a cold.'

Jack winced. Yet suddenly he heard another voice; it was his sister Dorothy, screaming at the fan: 'Leave my brother alone! He's doing his best.'

'Come on, our Jackie,' she cried. 'Play your heart out.'

Jack only had to glance round at the hopeful faces in the crowd to realize what defeat would mean. When the game halted for attention to the Pompey captain, Jack jogged upfield and beckoned the players to him.

'Right, lads,' he said, spitting on the ground. 'If any of you powder puffs want to lose, take my jersey and I'll play out. At least I'll run myself into the ground and bruise a few shins.'

No one took up his offer. But the mood changed. When the match restarted, the blue-shirted players fairly threw themselves into the game, chased every ball and tackled like terriers. Saints must have wondered what hit them.

Within five minutes the Pompey centre forward had scored—to the delight of the fans, who roared out the Pompey Chimes all round the ground. Fifteen minutes remained to draw level.

The burly No. 9, Charlie Weddle, hit the post with one pile-driver, headed against the bar when he should have scored, and then shot hopefully from a long way out. As luck would have it, the ball caught the heel of their centre half and was deflected into the corner of the net. 2–2.

The crowd went wild.

With one minute to go, the referee blew his whistle as Jack was challenged roughly in catching the ball. To everyone's astonishment, he was pointing to the spot. Penalty!

Even the Saints players seemed embarrassed at the decision.

Amid a cascade of boos, their captain cooly aimed hard and low for the corner. Yet Jack took off as if he had springs in his heels, caught the ball and, in one swift movement, threw it upfield to Harry.

With no one for support, Harry raced forward on his own. Three defenders stood between him and the goal. He tapped the ball through one man's legs and tore down the right wing, drawing the second defender. Then he cut inside to take on the other. As they came together in a sandwich from either side, he drew back the ball with his foot, flicked it up and over the defenders, then nipped in between them.

His speed took him through the tackle as they crashed into each other. That left him one-on-one with the goalie.

For a split second Jack thought Harry'd lost his nerve. Then he watched, heart in mouth, as the ball flew into the top corner of the net, past the goalkeeper's despairing lunge.

The fans danced and sang and cheered as if they'd won the war. Victory over the Saints: 3–2.

Harry and Jack were the heroes of the hour. Many were forecasting a brilliant future for the two talented youngsters. Future England stars . . .

Not everyone sang their praises. Far from it. When they turned up to backslaps and cheers at the drill hall on Monday evening, Colour Sergeant Jeffries was lying in wait. Captain Cleal was nowhere to be seen.

'You two erks,' shouted Jeffries, 'straight to the CO's office.'

Perhaps he'd prepared a little celebration to mark their footballing feats?

One look inside the office soon squashed that idea.

Captain Cleal was sitting bolt upright behind a desk. Though it was hot and stuffy, he was oddly wearing gloves; the leather belts across his chest were as glossy as conkers. Gingernob was flanked by two senior officers. One had a pink face, bushy white moustache, and a monocle; the other man was purple-faced and peered at them over the top of his spectacles. He reminded Jack of a short-sighted turkey cock.

Their former Head was the first to speak.

'Cadet Loveless, Cadet Newell. You have wilfully disobeyed orders and gone absent without leave. What do you have to say for yourselves?'

They could hardly believe their ears. Cleal and his buddies obviously weren't football fans. Or maybe they were secret Southampton supporters?

The two boys did their best to penetrate the thick skulls before them: it was an honour to play for Pompey, victory boosted the town's morale; they needed every ounce of strength for the match . . .

'Anyway, sir,' concluded Jack, 'pardon me for saying so, but we aren't in the Army and don't have to obey *your* orders.'

It was like talking to a brick wall.

From the stony faces opposite, it looked a safe bet they were going to be lined up against the wall and shot!

It was the old Walrus who replied in their defence. Unlike the dry voice of Ginger Cleal, his was foreign. Not foreign as in German or French. Foreign as in plummy, snooty, look-down-your-nose-at-dog-muck; foreign as in inhabiting a world of public schools, vicarages, and country houses.

In other words, an army officer.

If this was the type who was running the war, God help the poor beggers in the field!

'Look here, you chaps. It won't do. This is wartime. Our lads over there are fighting for King and Country. A few are dying at the hands of the filthy Hun. *Dulce et decorum est pro patria mori*—as Horace put it.'

Whoever this Horace was he obviously didn't speak good English, thought Jack.

It was Captain Cleal's happy duty to pronounce sentence.

'Cadet Loveless, Cadet Newell, you will be sent to Aldershot for a fortnight. A good dose of route marching with rifle and pack should make men of you. That is all. Dismiss.'

What a reward for saving a penalty and scoring the winning goal! thought Jack.

9

If you can keep your head when all about you
*   Are losing theirs and blaming it on you,*
If you can trust yourself when all men doubt you,
*   But make allowance for their doubting too;*
If you can wait and not be tired by waiting,
*   Or being lied about, don't deal in lies,*
Or being hated, don't give way to hating,
*   And yet don't look too good, nor talk too wise:*

* * *

If you can fill the unforgiving minute
*   With sixty seconds' worth of distance run,*
Yours is the Earth and everything that's in it,
*   And—which is more—you'll be a Man, my son!*

from 'If' by Rudyard Kipling

Who can explain it?

How does a boy who wouldn't hurt a fly become as hard as nails? How does a gentle soul turn into a mindless brute who obeys each order without a thought?

Wind him up and watch him go:

Quick march!

At the double!

Left, right, left, right . . .

Shoulder arms!

Shoot to kill!

It's odd how swiftly they can break you—and remake you.

They take away your clothes, down to your pants and socks, they dress you all alike in khaki brown, cut your hair as short as corn stubble, sleep you in rows of iron bunks, one up, one down, inside log barracks surrounded by barbed wire.

No way in, no way out, save under guard.

Rise and shine at five, before the dawn, wash and shave together in tin troughs of freezing water. Then off you go in full kit and pack on a five-mile run, boots clattering on roads still wet with dew. How welcome are that mug of cocoa and the doorstep of bread and plum jam for breakfast—same rations for all: the long and the short and the tall.

After breakfast, four hours of square bashing, rifle drill, and physical jerks. Aching bodies collapse on to canteen benches, each meal the same in billy cans and tin plates, wolfed down without a taste.

With fuel on board, the machine can run again, enough for thirty miles. Tea, then lectures till 6.30. Lights out at 9.15.

All day, every day. Only Sundays vary, with church parades instead of rifle drill. Blow what He said about putting your feet up on the Sabbath. There couldn't have been a war on then.

Within days, stripped of everything tying him to his former life, the Soldier surrenders. His eyes are dull and glazed, his brain shaken through his ear-holes and replaced by Colonel Frankenstein's pins and sawdust mixture.

He is ready for war, for marching into machine-gun fire.

God help those who resist.

The sergeant major makes life HELL. That's his job. He wants them to want to kill him. So he picks on the rebels, bellows in their ear for the entertainment of the rest.

'You snivelling coward, a baby tied to Mummy's apron strings. At first sight of Jerry, you'd run a mile, leave your comrades in the lurch. You'd turn your back and let the Hun kill your mother and little sisters . . . '

He'll have you back on the square, doubling round alone in greatcoat and pack until you drop.

He'll have you down on your knees, cutting grass with knife and fork, whitewashing the stones, polishing the guardroom floor until you see your face in it—then 'Do it again!', as he chucks down slops.

There's a limit to what a man can take; even the toughest have their breaking point. It's so much easier to give in. Oh, so much easier.

> Bless 'em all, bless 'em all,
> The long and the short and the tall.
> Bless all the sergeants and WOIs,
> Bless all the corporals and their blinking sons;
> 'Cos I'm saying goodbye to them all,
> As back to the billets they fall;
> You'll get no promotion, this side of the ocean,
> So, cheer up my lads, bless 'em all.

By the end of their fortnight at the Aldershot 'holiday camp', Jack and Harry were A1 soldiers. At least, both had passed all tests. They had been too tired to celebrate their seventeenth birthdays, their coming of age, their change from happy-go-lucky schoolboys to fighting men.

In the eyes of the brass hats, they'd done well. Being fit and sporty, they'd had the edge over the fat and flabby, the seedy and weedy. Better than most, they could shoot a rifle, climb ropes, run through mud, cut barbed wire, and wrestle opponents to the ground.

On the final day, Sergeant Major Blood did something they'd never thought him capable of. He smiled. He even spoke in almost human tones:

41

'Well done, laddies.'

By the time they got back home, their minds were made up.

They'd join up.

It had nothing to do with King and Country and hip-hip-hooray. Kitchener's finger didn't beckon them. They didn't believe the Germans would come over and kill their mothers and sisters. They weren't escaping to freedom and adventure, nor were they keen to be battle heroes.

No, though they couldn't put words to it, war had become a challenge—like playing in a big match, a test of their manhood, a chance to go and do something.

In any case, as Sergeant Major Blood had told them many times, 'If you don't join up, you'll miss all the fun. It'll be over and done with by Christmas.'

Without a word to their families, they went down to the Recruiting Office, signed on the dotted line and took the King's shilling.

You had to be nineteen to sign up. Yet the Recruiting Sergeant hadn't even asked their age. It was only later that afternoon, when they were lined up on Southsea Common, that the Colonel came round (that same monocled toff with the white walrus moustache) and asked their ages.

Aldershot must have put years on them, for he didn't recognize Jack or Harry.

'How old are you?' he asked Jack.

'Nineteen, sir.'

'And you?' he asked Harry.

'Nineteen, sir,' replied Harry, following Jack's lead.

He moved on to the next man, spoke to him, then came back to Harry.

'How old did you say you were?'

'Same as my pal Jack, sir,' said Harry. 'Nineteen.'

The Colonel stared hard, muttered something into his moustache, but walked on by.

After inspection, the Sergeant made a beeline for Harry and told him the Colonel hadn't believed him.

'Now, look here, young fellow-me-lad. We're leaving for France tomorrow and we don't want you bawling your eyes out over there, saying you miss your mummy. It'll be too late then, so make up your mind.'

'I'm going with Jack,' said Harry.

'Right, lads. Report to the Town Station tomorrow morning at ten.'

Jack's mum and dad weren't happy at all. His father blamed the government. His mum just sat and cried. Jack did his best to comfort her.

'Don't worry, Mum. I'll be back soon. Harry and I'll watch out for each other.'

Harry's mum went wild and slapped his face.

'That'll larn you to go and join the army,' she screamed

His dad sighed and held his tongue, secretly wishing he had the courage to enlist.

Both families were glad of the money. While Harry's mother took away his shilling, Jack's mum kept only ninepence, leaving him and Harry enough for a packet of five Woodbines and a box of matches.

They lit up, inhaled the smoke like grown men—and coughed and spluttered like schoolboys.

And off they went to war.

10

Jack walked to the Town Station early on Thursday morning. He was all done up smartly in uniform: stiff round hat, khaki jacket and trousers, pack on his back with rolled-up ground-sheet on top. Handsome enough to turn girls' heads.

'There goes Jack Loveless. Don't he look grand!'

His mum and dad insisted on coming too; Doss stayed home with the kids, but Floss marched proudly at her big brother's side, holding on to his hand. Like a mother hen, Jack's mum fussed over her first-born.

'Got your toothbrush, Jack? I've put a warm scarf and woollies in your bag. It'll be cold and draughty over there in them trenches. Make sure you eat decent; don't scoff your food. I've packed some arrowroot biscuits and two sticks of barley sugar. Keep yerself clean, you know what they say: cleanliness is next to godliness.'

At first Jack smiled kindly on the mollycoddling and cheering, but after a while he couldn't wait to board the troop train. Harry wasn't to be seen anywhere. As the homely party got closer to the station, they joined up like rivulets into a stream of other families.

Crowds were lining the streets, bulging on corners, jam-packing the pavements around the station. They were mostly women, waving, worrying, weeping.

'Good luck, boys.'

'Cheerio, lads.'

'Come back soon.'

To his surprise, Jack heard one woman strike a different note.

44

'Poor little beggars. Fancy sending them to France to die for us.'

That jolted him. He wasn't going to die for anyone. He wanted to shake her: he *definitely* wasn't going to die, for her or anyone else.

He was anxious in case Mum or Floss had overheard. It was Dad, however, who was most down in the mouth. Unlike the others, he had a clear view beyond the flowers, the cheers, the flag-waving. He saw men crouching behind sandbags, burrowing into trench walls, disintegrating into scraps of flesh, booted feet, blackened hands, eyeless heads.

But Dad never gave word to his grim thoughts; they just squeezed out in bitter tears, like drops of lemon juice.

At the station, Jack's mum flung her arms round him, and out gushed the now unblocked stream of tears. She *had* heard the moaning minny along the way, for she suddenly mumbled through her sobs, 'If you don't come back . . .'

Impatiently, Jack stopped her before she could finish.

'Don't fret, Mum, I *will* be back!'

Then, more softly, he added with a smile, 'Pompey needs me.'

Floss squeezed his hand and pleaded, 'Make sure you write.'

Dad simply said 'Good luck, son' and turned quickly away.

Jack broke off to join the train queue; to his surprise he found himself behind a boy he'd known at school— Freddie Feltham—a tubby, cheerful lad who was always being ribbed by staff and pupils alike. They'd been pals ever since Jack had stood up for him against school bullies.

Freddie's mother, a roly-poly, dumpy woman, was

45

clinging to her only son. She'd obviously been crying all day long—her face was puffy and blotchy. All this fuss clearly miffed Freddie, even more so when she grabbed Jack's arm and begged him to keep an eye on her 'darling baby boy'.

Jack gave her his word he'd do his best, though he wondered how you keep an eye on someone in a battle charge.

As they boarded the train, Jack finally caught sight of Harry, hopping on the last carriage. He was only just in time because the old puffer hooted, bilious clouds of steam rose up, mercifully blocking out the waving crowds, and the train creaked and cranked into motion.

Is there anything more mournful than a station groaning with departing troops?

It took only half an hour to reach Southampton Docks, time enough for Jack to squeeze down eight corridors crammed with raw recruits. The air was blue and sour with cigarette smoke as the young men puffed nervously on their parting gifts.

At last, soaked in sweat, Jack made the final carriage and was surprised to find Harry had a seat—not on the hard cushions, but up on the luggage rack, his red face pressed hard against the cat's-cradle string. Like Freddie Feltham, the train was bursting at the seams.

The sailing wasn't till nightfall: they were to slip out in the dead of night: enemy subs were lurking in the Channel, like sharks hungry for prey.

So the Pompey privates had time on their hands before bidding goodbye to Blighty. Thanks to army muddle, hour upon hour was spent standing in long queues for food, toilets and, finally, boarding the troop ship.

The three George Street old boys waited on the quayside in the drizzling autumn rain. Looming above them was the *Aragon*, a Royal Mail Steam Packet liner commandeered by the Royal Navy and turned into a troop ferry boat.

As the straggly line of men in greatcoats, with full packs on their backs, waited in the rain, they suddenly heard a strange, far-off rumbling sound, a mummummummummummum, now and then punctured by a boommoommoommoomm.

'What the blooming heck's that?' asked Harry.

'That's the Western Front, mush,' said a passing corporal.

The distant rumble grew as they embarked and weighed anchor, passing Blockhouse Fort and the Nab Lighthouse before entering the Channel. All lights on board were dimmed and all portholes shut tight. Hundreds of men were stacked into the ship, squeezed together below deck or lying up top, under strict orders not to show a light, especially from cigarettes. In any case, many were too seasick to smoke, even on the short trip to France.

The whole ship soon stank of vomit and stale piss.

As the *Aragon* left port, it was joined by two escort cruisers, one Japanese, the other Russian. The latter oddly sported five funnels—so it soon got dubbed the Packet of Woodbines.

Jack had been sick all the way across the Channel, lying on deck spewing his guts up. Even when they got into Boulogne, he still felt like death warmed up. It was four in the morning, pouring with rain and just getting light as the long line of soldiers trudged up the cobblestone high street, all the way to Bull Ring Camp above the town.

At the sound of tramping feet, the windows of some houses went up and bleary-eyed women and children poked out their heads, shouting a cheery welcome:

'Bienvenue, les anglais!'

''Ello, Tommy!'

Once they reached the hilltop, the Hampshire 'hogs' were put six to a bell tent at the very edge of the sprawling camp. This was to be home for the next few days, until orders arrived to send them 'up the line'.

There were no beds, not even straw palliasses. Jack and his mates had to sleep on groundsheets, covering themselves with their greatcoats. Even under canvas, they were ankle-deep in mud. Every day it rained in torrents or, as the local French said delicately, like cows pissing.

The ground was so heavy and waterlogged, you soon couldn't tell new recruits from old sweats. All were soaking wet, stinking to high heaven, and lousy with half-drowned lice.

All the men got to eat each morning was a couple of hard tack biscuits and a hunk of cheese; that was meant to last them for the rest of the day. 'All the decent grub's sent to the Front field kitchens,' they were told.

It was a stark choice: stay put and starve to death, or go to the Front and die on a full stomach.

The instructors were rumoured to be rejects from home training camps; that was why they took their revenge on the newcomers, knocking steam out of them. All day long, Jack and his comrades did 'war' training—attacking mock trenches, jumping over obstacles, slogging and crawling on their bellies through treacly, stinking mud.

Poor Freddie was the 'darling' of the PT instructors: he didn't get out of the trenches fast enough—so they shoved him back, time and time again. One angry sergeant blamed the entire tent for Freddie's failings; he poked his head through the flaps one night and shouted, 'When Jerry sees your lovely pink faces and fat arses, he'll rub his hands and say "*Mein Gott*, rat-tat-tat, ze English boys, rat-tat-tat-tat".'

Freddie, the mild-mannered choirboy, who never smoked or swore, surprised everyone by vowing to shoot 'the bugger' first chance he got.

11

On their third day in France the men of the 15th Hants were woken in the dead of night by a noise like swarms of monster gnats. At first Jack hadn't the foggiest what it was: he'd never heard the whirring of mono-planes before.

When the skies opened and bombs rained down— dropped by hand from the planes—it was too late to wonder.

Pandemonium. Teeming rain.

Pitch darkness. Deafening explosions.

Screams. Blood-curdling screams.

For the first time in his life Jack felt the chill hand of death. Lying on the heaving ground, his eardrums blasted through his skull, he pulled the greatcoat over his head and lost his fight to stem the tide.

It was the first time he'd cried in years.

He wasn't the only one.

Through the thick dank serge, he heard blubbing, teeth chattering, flesh trembling like sheets flapping on a clothes line. Freddie was mumbling a prayer:

> 'Merciful Jesus, meek and mild,
> Pray protect your little child.'

Harry was calling for his mother and sobbing so hard it set the others off even more. If it hadn't been for a bold soul outside the tent they'd have dug a hole and burrowed all the way to China.

'Come on, lads,' the voice yelled. 'All hands on deck. Men are dying, they need help.'

It was like a bucket of icy water dashed into their faces.

They struggled to their feet, thankful that the darkness hid the shame of wet cheeks. Since no one undressed for the night, all they had to do was pull on boots and greatcoats, and jam down hats.

Following the panicky rush through sticky mud, Jack and the others soon realized that Jerry had hit the bull's-eye of Bull Ring Camp and skittled back to Jerryland.

The camp's defences—rifles firing into the air—hadn't scored a single hit. Under low rainclouds the gunners could only hear, not see, their targets. The Very lights fizzled out like damp squibs; their thin glare was no more than a wavy chalk line on an enormous blackboard. It was like firing a popgun at a moth in a darkened room.

All that was left of the centre of the camp was a great gaping hole of sludge. Through the rainy gloom Jack could hear and dimly see water leaking out of the earth, as through a sieve, into a rapidly-filling crater.

Someone still alive at the bottom was working his arms like mad, jerking his head and gurgling for help. But the water was rising above his head, and finally all that remained were bubbles floating on top, like frogspawn.

There was no way anyone could slide into the crater to save him.

Soon, a greeny-brown shroud of slimy water covered the dead. All about the bomb-hole, however, were scenes of horror starkly lit up by scores of lamps. The bombs had flattened the camp stores, stables, and command posts. If Jerry had hoped to kill fighting men, he'd drawn a blank. The dead and dying were cooks, medical orderlies, instructors, and horses.

Worst of all to witness were the wounded horses. It was heart-rending to hear a horse, crazed with pain, screaming in its death throes. Thankfully, Jack soon heard single shots ring out, signalling a death squad putting the poor beasts out of their misery.

The mercy mission was not lost on some dying men.

As Jack and Freddie stood together shivering, staring down into the black pit of death, they heard whimpers to one side. Following the low moaning, they stumbled upon two badly-wounded men lying in a pool of blood.

The first had been blinded: one eye was hanging from its socket, the other had been torn out. If that weren't bad enough, he had also lost a leg, and it was blood from an artery that was pumping out into the pool.

The second was even further gone. The poor devil had no face, an arm had been blown off, and what looked like a string of red-raw chitterlings was dangling from his stomach.

The first begged for help.

'Don't let me die, son. I'm badly hurt. Help, help me.'

The other, evidently knowing he was at death's door, called out to Freddie. It was something the chubby ex-choirboy least expected.

'You useless fat prat, for Christ's sake do something right for a change! Put a bullet in me.'

As calm as you like, Freddie slowly bent down and unhooked the revolver from under the man's spilled guts. Jack watched aghast as Freddie stood up straight, then fired into the mangled head.

Not from hatred or anger. Just from pity, like putting down a dying horse.

Bang! It was all over.

The head jerked back, added more gore to the sticky pool, and the body lay still.

'Sorry, Sarge,' Freddie muttered.

It was the first man he'd killed.

The officers had escaped without even a headache: at the time of the bombs they'd been fast asleep in their feather beds at the chateau down the hill.

When, just after dawn, a party of officers arrived to take

command, they quickly sized up the damage. The bombs had certainly done their work. Corpses of men, carcasses of horses, mangled lorries, and cooking stoves were all strewn about water-filled craters in the centre of the camp.

The Commanding Officer had all the men lined up and, in front of everyone, calmly gave the gunners a dressing down for slack work. Someone had to take the blame. Then, handing over to junior officers, he went off for coffee and a croissant.

'Carry on, men.'

What bodies—or bloodied bits of bloodied bodies—that could be found were stretchered away to the wooded slope of the hill. Parties of men dug a long trench in the marshy soil, while others wrapped the human remains in army blankets and neatly stacked them into the ditch.

The trouble was, the deeper they dug, the more the burial trench filled up with muddy water, so that the bodies began to shift and sit up, like zombies rising from the grave.

After the floating corpses had been hastily covered with soggy soil, the whole camp was lined up for the funeral service. A bare-headed chaplain in white surplice chanted a few phrases in a sing-song voice that few could understand, and a boy bugler played the Last Post. Those lucky enough to have real guns reversed arms, and half a dozen riflemen fired a salvo into the air.

The rain poured down like torrents of tears upon the mourners.

12

If in some smothering dreams, you too could pace
Behind the wagon that we flung him in,
And watch the white eyes writhing in his face,
His hanging face, like a devil's sick of sin;
If you could hear, at every jolt, the blood
Come gargling from the froth-corrupted lungs,
Obscene as cancer, bitter as the cud
Of vile, incurable sores on innocent tongues,—
My friend, you would not tell with such high zest
To children ardent for some desperate glory,
The old Lie: Dulce et decorum est
Pro patria mori.

       from 'Dulce et Decorum est' by Wilfred Owen

Jack's first letter home

10 October 1914
Dear Floss

    I'm sitting here in a café drinking coffee. You wouldn't think there's a war on. If it weren't for the non-stop thundery noise outside like an orchestra of kettle drums, I could be in Joe's café down Albert Road. At the tables round me are half a dozen old fogies with sticks, too old to go to war, too young to miss the joys of life. Behind the bar there's a couple of chirpy Oooh-la-la girls, giving me the glad eye. Life goes on, even in wartime.

    We're on our way up the line, and it's a bit scary, I can tell you. After the Jerries bombed our camp, we had to move out in a hurry. 'Better die in battle than die in wait,' some wag said. But I'm not going to die, don't worry. I haven't seen hair or hide of Hansie Hun yet.

It's funny, some villages we go through are knocked bandy, others haven't a scratch on them. Mind you, I've seen enough in the past few days to last a lifetime. One thing I've learned: nothing lasts forever in this topsy-turvy world.

No one lasts forever either.

This part of France has seen a lot of scrapping. It's see-sawed to and fro since war began. First the Boche moves forward, we drive him back. He counter attacks, gains fifty yards, we drive him back forty. He advances seventy, we push him back eighty.

What price a patch of earth, eh? Hundred bodies to a square yard, I reckon.

The other day we stumbled upon a big white tent like a marquee. For all the world it looked like one of those Easter circuses we get on Southsea Common. It didn't look military at all. Other men must have thought the same because we all rushed up as if we smelt sawdust and elephant dung, keen to see high wire acrobats and red-nosed clowns in baggy trousers.

When we pulled open the flaps, what did we see?!

Row upon row of dead Germans, their eyes wide open, staring at us in astonishment. They must have copped it at the start of the war, and been lying there for a couple of months. The rats had already had a right old feast!

Funny thing death: most of the flesh had gone from the face, yet the hair and beard had still grown. It was blinking awful. When you touched a body the rats came tumbling out of the chest, ever so cross at being turfed out of their beds. You can't blame them, I suppose; the ribcage made a cosy old nest for them. And they certainly weren't short of grub.

If you're a rat, a nest's a nest. But it was terrible to think that some young bloke was providing rats with a roof over their heads. Oo-er, it gives me the creeps just writing about it.

What with hundreds of rats running over the bodies, the disgusting stench of rotting corpses, and the half-eaten flesh, I felt like running a mile. But someone had to cope, and it's amazing how quickly you become accustomed to death and suffering.

Sergeant Hickey detailed our section to bury the dead, give them a decent Christian burial.

It was no easy job, but it had its funny side (if you don't laugh, you might as well turn up your toes). Well, we shovelled them into a ditch. The trouble was that bits kept sticking out like a badly-made bed. Stiff arms were the worst. They'd poke out of the earth we shovelled over them, and start pointing, praying, even waving to us!

Gave me the heeby-jeebies.

There was one grubby hand sticking up in the air . . . We all shook it when we passed by, saying, 'Good morning, Kaiser Bill,' in a posh voice. It was just a bit of bravado to hide our fear.

I had to keep reminding myself that these dead strangers were the Enemy; I shouldn't be feeling sorry for them. But I did. They had come to France like us, thought they were there to do a job, reckoned their cause was just . . . And WHAM!

Their war was over in a split second. They'll never see their families again, poor blighters.

I heard later that twenty thousand men had been killed on both sides in a single day! Jesus, what a waste. Has any war in the history of the world done for so many so quickly? I must ask Mr Hitchens the history teacher when I get back.

After the burial, I had to take their paybooks back down the line. At Brigade Headquarters I went down some steps into a deep bunker dug in the chalky ground. After what I'd just been through the posh living quarters there made me feel queasy.

I was given a cup of tea from a china cup, with real milk! As I was drinking it I noticed a box of cakes on the table—labelled Fortnum and Mason, Piccadilly. What nosh! For some reason it made me think of the poor dead German lads, and I couldn't wait to get back to my mates sheltering in rickety old cowsheds.

It hurts me just to talk about it, but I've got to share it with someone. The other day we took a prisoner. We found him wandering about lost, after they'd pulled back. He looked ever so young, poor lad, a country boy from a farm in Bavaria. Funny thing was he spoke the lingo well. He said his mum had taught him so's he could give himself up to us at the first opportunity.

She said we'd look after him, see him right till the end of the war, then he could go home to his pigs and cows. He was a hefty lad with a ruddy open face. The blokes all came to have a dekko at him—they'd never seen a live Jerry before—and give him chocolate.

This 'Little Willy', as we called him, kept

clutching his side, complaining of a pain at the back of his hip. When our medical orderly went to patch him up, he found the wound more serious than the poor lad realized. A jagged piece of shrapnel was lodged in his hip and gangrene had set in. You could smell it.

'He needs urgent treatment at base hospital,' said Jimmy, our medical orderly.

In a quiet aside to us, he said, 'If he doesn't get it soon he'll be a goner.'

But our CO wouldn't hear of it.

'The boy must be interrogated first,' he said. 'Captain Smithers (evidently an old school pal of his) will give him a thorough going over, winkle secrets out of him that could save the lives of our chaps. What's their company strength? What sort of weapons can they muster? How's morale? That sort of thing.'

The 'Three Musketeers', that's me, Harry, and Freddie Feltham, were detailed to take our precious POW to the intelligence post where some officers spoke German.

It was over two miles back to the post, up and down ravines, through heavy mire and squelchy fields. The poor wounded lad was bleeding badly and found it heavy going. I had to put my arm round his shoulders to help him along. All the same, he put a brave face on it, asking us about England: was it always foggy? What was school like? What sort of prison camp would he go to? Could he do something useful on a farm?

He told us about his own life on the farm, milking cows, making cheese and butter, mushrooming in the Black Forest, how he'd joined a Pathfinder youth group with other boys and, next thing he knew, the whole lot had been signed on as messenger boys.

It reminded me of how Harry and I had got roped in.

We got quite pally. In that small space of foreign soil we came to see him as a brother, a mother's son like us; we didn't think of him as enemy.

Not so the intelligence officers. Oh dear no! We handed him over to Captain Smithers and were told to wait outside.

With a smile and wave to us, 'Little Willy' disappeared down the tunnel, while we sat up top, having a smoke. That was the last we saw of the poor devil.

I got quite a shock when I heard this big bang. It made us all jump. Surely it wasn't what we thought it was?

Next thing we know, this captain comes up with a smoking revolver in his hand, wiping it on his sleeve.

'I never knew Germans had so many brains,' he remarked to us with a smile.

When he saw our horror-stricken expressions, he muttered, 'It'll save you the bother of taking him back. He'd have died of his wounds anyway. You'll learn, chaps: the only good German's a dead German.'

War certainly teaches you about life and people.

Dear Sis, that's all for now. Sorry my letter's a bit gruesome. That's war for you, it's no picnic, that's for sure.

The main thing is that I'm in the pink. So's

Harry and Freddie (who used to have a crush on you!!!). Don't worry about me.

Remember me to everyone. Write as soon as you can. DON'T FORGET!!!

With love and kisses, ta-ta for now. God bless.

Your ever loving brother,

Jack

PS If you can, send me one of your cakes please.

13

Two months had passed since Jack and his platoon had arrived in France. Still no action. The lads were restless, like bulls pawing the ground before a bullfight; they were sick to the back teeth of mindless drill, drill, drill.

Every day, troops passed through the village.

Some one way, some the other.

Young, eager, hopeful faces looking east. Old, tired, haggard faces looking nowhere.

The eastward marchers chattered like magpies, laughed and sang: 'Onward, Christian so-ol-diers, marching as to war; With the cross of Jesus, marching on before . . .'

The westward men were as silent as death.

What had they seen to stamp out the spark of life?

They would not tell.

All that one or two would say through clenched teeth was, 'You'll see.'

It was like a schoolboy returning from a caning, biting his lip.

Their silence only fuelled the curiosity of the innocent. The support troops couldn't wait to have a taste of action, take a pot at Jerry. Not for death and glory, not for any cross of Jesus. Far from it. They just wanted to do something worthwhile, see some action.

There was so much they didn't understand.

An upset occurred that confused them even more.

It was late November and Jack and Harry were on sentry duty. A cold biting wind was blowing a drizzling rain into their faces. As evening drew on, the rain couldn't make up its mind: should it take pity on the warriors and glister them with soft, silvery snowflakes? Or should it pelt the killers with hailstones?

Unsure, it turned in-between, to sleet.

Suddenly, tramping feet were heard and six figures slowly took shape out of the gloom. Friend, not foe, judging by their fish-plate helmets. One, in the middle, was bare-headed and staring straight ahead.

'Another Jerry prisoner by the look of it,' said Harry.

But he was wrong.

By the time Jack and Harry went off duty and retired to their ruined stone barn, the prisoner was sitting in one corner, arms hugging his knees, still staring blankly ahead.

The corporal in charge was passing round dixie cans of stew, and the rum ration. Although the prisoner was offered both, he wouldn't eat or drink; he just sat there, unhearing, unseeing, unaware of anything about him.

By the look of him, he was no older than Jack, though his sunken eyes added another twenty years to his face.

The cup that cheers obviously worked its magic and oiled the corporal's tongue. He felt the need to talk, turning the air blue with strong language, getting it out of his system. He found a ready audience in the Hampshire lads.

The dumb man was a deserter, 'bloody craven coward' in the corporal's words. Perhaps the words weren't really his because his tale and tone betrayed more sympathy than contempt.

'Up and over, says the major. And up and over it is, me boys, if the major says so. Effin' daft order, if you asks me. Straight down the throat of the Hun's machine guns. Flippin' suicide it were.

'Young matey 'ere, he done 'is bloody best. By rights he should be 'angin' on the bleedin' wire like his dead chums. But he survives. Then what does 'e go and bloody well do?'

The corporal looked questioningly at his audience, as if they already knew the answer.

'Chucks down 'is effin' rifle and scarpers . . . right into the waiting arms of the officer chappie, sheltering in the trench. Instead of a hug and kiss, he gets court-martialled, don't 'e? Poor little bugger, e's only seventeen, still wet behind the soddin' ears.'

With a sigh and long drag on his fag, he spat out the next words with the tobacco smoke.

'He'll be shot at dawn.'

All the while, the 'poor little bugger' sat staring into space. What did he see? What did he feel? What was he thinking on his last night on earth?

No one would ever know.

It was a messy business. First the officer was late, and the lad had to stand in the drizzle for over an hour, tied to the execution post by the barn wall.

The war-weary corporal said, as if reading from the Bible, 'Army regulations state: only an officer can supervise an execution.'

When two executioners drove up, the senior officer got to work right away. He gave his subaltern a running commentary, like a hospital surgeon breaking in a new student.

The condemned man had to be blindfolded.

'No, a handkerchief won't do,' he barked, pointing his stick at the corporal. 'Put a sack over his head.'

'Covers his whole head,' he commentated in a loud voice, 'so the men can't see the face twitching. It can put 'em orff. Stuff the mouth with cotton wool,' he shouted to the corporal.

There wasn't any. Corporal Skinner volunteered an old rag he'd used for cleaning his rifle.

The senior officer nodded curtly and turned to his fellow officer.

'Some of 'em kick up one hell of a fuss—praying, hollering, blubbing, don't you know. We had to put a stop to that, puts the firing squad orff. Now we shut 'em up.'

Despite his careful preparations, the officer was wasting his time. For the prisoner was as docile as a lamb. He bent this way and that with each tug and shove.

The entire barnful of men had turned out for the spectacle. Not from choice. But at the officer's command.

'*Pour encourager les autres,*' he said, with a knowing look towards 'Guy Fawkes'. He seemed to regard all the men as potential deserters who'd choose to flee given half a chance.

All was now ready.

The body was slumped against the post, hands tied firmly behind his back, the sack covering his face.

The detail of five lined up, ten paces from the limp figure, rifles at the ready.

Suddenly, the condemned man came to life, as if waking from a deep sleep. His head started to jerk madly, his arms and shoulders shook violently, trying to break free, his knees sagged. If that weren't bad enough, an eerie sound came from his throat:

'Aaarrraaa. Aaarrraaa!'

'FIRE!'

But the rifles wavered. Only one bullet hit the mark, one out of five, and that in the shoulder.

'The bastard's not even stunned,' muttered the captain.

'Jolly poor show,' said the major in sympathy.

Not trusting the men to finish the job, the gloved officer prodded the major with his stick.

'Right, Lewinson. Usual routine. March the men orff.

Revolver well into mouth, muzzle slightly upwards. Finish it off, there's a good chap.'

It was soon done.

Jack stared at the blood-spattered wall, closed his eyes and, without as much as by your leave, was violently sick all over a wet clump of dandelions.

Next day the platoon was sent to the Front.

What a blessed relief!

14

'O Jesus Christ!' one fellow sighed.
And kneeled, and bowed, tho' not in prayer, and died.
  And the Bullets sang 'In Vain',
  Big Guns guffawed 'In Vain'.

'Father and mother!' one boy said.
Then smiled—at nothing, like a small child; being dead.
  And the Shrapnel Cloud
  Slowly gestured 'Vain',
  The falling splinters muttered 'Vain'.

'My love!' another cried, 'My love, my bud!'
Then gently lowered, his whole face kissed the mud.
  And the Flares gesticulated, 'Vain',
  The Shells hooted, 'In Vain',
  And the Gas hissed, 'In Vain'.

from 'Last Words' by Wilfred Owen

The mood was jaunty as Jack's platoon moved out that late November morning. It was only a ten-day stint: ten days in the trenches, ten days in reserve. At least that was the plan.

'Decent grub at last,' sighed Freddie. 'I'm starved.'

'Yeah, and double rum ration,' added Harry.

'How we'll miss dear old Sarge,' laughed Jack.

They all sang out together:

> 'Kiss me goodnight, Sergeant Major,
> Tuck me in my little wooden bed.'

66

They would not have felt so cocky had they known that most of the platoon would not last ten days . . .

Their bravado began to wear thin the closer they got to the battlefield. The gunfire rose to thunder pitch, each explosion made them wince. Not only that: they now had to plough through a jungle of bomb craters, shell-holes, rutted gulleys, and fields littered with nasty war mementos—barbed wire, green slime tinged with red, army tunics and boots, sometimes with owner attached, face down—if any face remained.

The going got even worse as they jumped down into a communication trench leading to the front line. The water and mud were knee deep, and panic-stricken rats, their hairy snouts poking above the waterline, dog-paddled past or scuttled along the parapet. The stench of rotting dead clogged their nostrils as they reached a crossroad; under the cloudy greyness, a signboard flapped crookedly in the wind.

'This Way To Hell,' it said.

From now on the trenches grew more cramped; sandbags were torn to shreds, so that sand dribbled down and half filled the trench. Sometimes they had to halt and wriggle a way past the file of men they were replacing— some who groaned and cried out in pain as they limped along; others who hurried to escape, pale or crimsoned by fever.

No greeting, no words of thanks, no 'Best of luck, mate'.

Just a straggling silent herd taking flight in a panic of fear and shock, their feet pulling up huge clumps of mud in the mad rush to get away.

The section of front line detailed for Jack's platoon resembled a graveless graveyard.

Bodies were stuffed into the parapet like makeshift sandbags, feet often overarching the trench, so that you had to dodge underneath as you passed. On the sole of one stray foot, someone had chalked 'Taffy. RIP'. Less considerate was a tin mug hung on a stiff finger crooked like a hook.

Thank goodness it was midday, when the guns were silent.

'Keep your head down!' shouted the platoon commander, a lanky chinless wonder fresh out of Winchester where officers grow on trees—then, at the first whiff of gunsmoke, drop like rotten fruit.

'If you poke your head up, snipers will blow it off.'

It was one of those useless commands, like 'Don't piss into the wind' or 'Fall down if you're dead'.

Nothing could have prepared Jack and his comrades for the Front.

'You ain't seen nuffin' yet,' said Sergeant Misery Guts, noticing the pale faces and shaking hands. All the same, since they'd not yet experienced shellfire or, worse still, gone over the top, they still retained an innocent cheeriness. For the moment they vented their ire on the enemy within—the lice and the rats.

Lice itched, soldiers scratched. The men spent hours 'chatting'—popping lice and their eggs in hair and tunic seams. But those nasty 'little soldiers of the night' always won the war. You would kill hundreds and find hundreds still.

As for the rats, Freddie put it in a nutshell: 'Well, we live like rats, so we might as well get used to living with the blighters!'

The greedy beasts were everywhere. If you dropped a biscuit, there'd be half a dozen of them fighting over it. Like ant or woodlice racing, it helped to pass the time.

It was strange really. After all, the rats had so much dead flesh to gobble. Sergeant Hickey hissed a dire warning, 'Watch out for the Hun. Right now he's digging a tunnel underneath you. And all at once—'Boo!'—he'll pop up behind you and, Bang-Bang!, you'll be feeding them rats.'

A couple of Simple Simons fell flat on their bellies, one ear to the ground. Sure enough, they could hear the tip-tap, tip-tap of picks and shovels down below.

'You're dead right, Sarge. I can 'ear 'em!'

Sergeant Hickey turned away; it didn't do for the men to see him smile.

'It's rats burrowing underground and gnawing bones,' someone told the scared men.

You never knew when Sarge was pulling your leg. He swore that rats knew when a bombardment was due. 'Five minutes before the balloon goes up, they'll go scampering off. Wise old birds, them rats.'

Not that the men needed the Rat Alarm. Old Jerry was as regular as clockwork.

Bang on ten o'clock that night he struck up the band.

'Dead dependable, old Jerry,' said the sergeant. 'Does everything by numbers. One minute to fart, two to piss, three to shit. Wouldn't surprise me if he gives his missus one in five minutes flat.'

The concert opened with a whistling fanfare and short roll on the drums. Then a small red dot appeared in the sky's black safety curtain. The dot grew bigger and closer until the curtain rose in a blaze of light and sound.

It was a trench mortar, a *Minenwerfer*, or Minny Werfer as the men called it—one of the trillions of bits of iron the armies threw at each other. This one landed just short of the trenches, deafening and blinding, burying the nearest men under a seething mountain of smoke and earth.

A flying soldier churned the air with his arms like the conductor of the band. It was grotesque. He landed upright in No Man's Land; it was as if he'd taken root like a

69

screaming oak tree. Mercifully the newly-planted tree was quickly sawn in half by a hail of bullets. The trunk and two branches toppled over, while the stump stood firm in the ground.

Jack stared in horror at the first death in the platoon. He knew the dead man, a nice quiet chap who worked as a cobbler down Queen Street, just by the Hard.

There was no time to reflect on shoe repairs, for a whizz-bang came hurtling through the air with a ZUPPPPPPP, WHOOOSH, and BANG—and that was it. The sound was like sitting at an express train window when another whizzes by.

The force of the shell's explosion knocked Jack to the duckboards. The air was full of dust and smoke that scorched his throat and nose. As he sat there dumbly, counting his four limbs and looking fearfully for blood, he heard a brief cry down the line.

He stared open-mouthed as a piece of shell sliced the man's head completely off. It was all so unreal, the stuff of nightmares.

There was the headless body still pointing its rifle at the Hun, while its head watched the body from under someone's feet a yard away.

High in the dark sky, red and white flares suddenly appeared, rose up, coughed, sneezed, and disappeared. They had come from behind the lines, and were followed by the whump and whoosh of The Reply.

Two can play at that game. All night long, toe to toe, tit for tat, they slugged it out, both sides bloodied and groggy, yet neither willing to throw in the towel.

Shells whistled and banged, machine guns chattered and sputtered, flares zoomed up and fizzled down, stretcher bearers scurried like ferrets back and forth, cleaning up the mess, removing unsightly hunks of flesh.

Then, all at once, it stopped.

Jerry had gone for a cup of tea. As if by some pact, Tommy downed tools too. Time for a break. It was no more than a lull in the storm.

'Check your watches, lads,' Sergeant Hickey yelled. 'Forty-five minutes, not a second more. Dependable, those Huns. Time enough for a smoke and a catnap.'

He obviously admired German order.

So it went on until, dead on six-thirty, as the sun scowled disapprovingly over the horizon, the firing ceased and the men stood down.

It had been the longest night in Jack's life. The Three Musketeers had got through it somehow. As Sarge said, 'Them shells didn't have your names on 'em.'

But they did carry twenty-eight names that night. Thirteen poor beggars met their Maker, another fifteen were badly wounded.

Some price to pay for a night's work.

15

I'm war. Remember me?
'Yes, you're asleep,' you say, 'and you kill men.'
Look in my game-bag, fuller than you think.

I kill marriages.
If one dies, one weeps and then heals clean.
(No scar without infection.) That's no good.
I can do better when I really try . . .

I kill families.
Cut off the roots, the plant will root no more . . .

I am the game that nobody can win.
What's yours is mine, what's mine is still my own.
I'm War. Remember me.

    from 'Achtung! Achtung!' by Mary Hacker

Jack knew it was his lucky day.

Day Six, the first day of December, Mum's birthday—and he remembered his 'Rabbits', the first word he uttered, just after midnight. Now *nothing* would harm him. He could walk bare-chested towards the enemy and bullets would bounce off, like peas from a peashooter.

After all the killing, he didn't believe in a god; but Luck was different. You had to believe in Luck. What else *was* there to believe in?

As always, it came up trumps.

Late that morning the postman arrived. Rather, a

fatigue party came up with dixies of stew, boxes of ammo, and . . . parcels and letters from home.

'Private J. Loveless—one letter, one parcel.'

He tore the heavy envelope open with trembling fingers. His lopsided grin expressed joy and relief as he recognized Floss's bold scrawl and little matchstick drawings down the side.

No date: just 'Tuesday evening'. Place: 'Portsmouth.' Where else? Jack sighed and read the letter.

Dear Jack,

I'm sending you a letter and cake with some socks Dossie knitted. We send our love and trust you are well. We are well too. We got your letter and everyone has read it a million times. I read it to Gran cos her eyes aren't up to it. She must think you're in Africa cos she said to tell you to keep out of the way of them spears. Anyway, we're all thinking of you.

Now about us. Dad's so busy he only comes home to sleep. Mum's working, packing and sending food to the troops, earning a few bob to make ends meet. Doss and I run the house, cooking dinner—whopping great pots of stew and rice, sewing and darning clothes, ironing, bathing the kids, blacking the grate, scrubbing the doorstep, running errands. You soon learn. I get sixpenny-worth of bones from Sam Bartram the butcher, bung them in the pot with leeks and spuds, thicken it with barley—and hocus-pocus, there's your meal.

Lots of girls are doing war work, making guns and ammo, driving trams and trains, nursing, that sort of thing. Some of my friends have gone to work on farms, even joined the

73

police. Bet you've never seen a woman Bobby (Betty?) before.

With you bossy-boots out of the way, we girls can show we're as good as you (better even!). Mind you, them old fogies don't give in easy. I read that thousands of women paraded in London the other day, demanding the 'right to serve'. The government had to give in cos they need us to do the dirty work. They only give us half a man's wage, mingy devils—a pound a week for forty-eight hours. Old skinflints.

Mary next door's a Canary Girl. They call them that cos their skin goes all yellow from filling shells with TNT. Dodgy stuff. But they've got to do their bit, haven't they? The other day a pal of hers, Carol Reynolds, had her eyes blown out when the stuff exploded in her face. She had such pretty blue eyes too. I hear that some factory caught fire up in London. Seventy poor devils got fried. But don't you fret. They'll be fine.

Ever such a lot of men are joining up. They can't get their hands on the King's shilling quick enough. An schoolfriend of mine, he's only fifteen, went to sign on and they asked him how old he was. He went and told the truth. This sergeant, he says 'Go for a walk round Victoria Park. When you come back you'll be nineteen.' So he did, took his shilling and signed up.

Not everyone's that keen. But if people see a chap on the street, they say 'Why aren't you in the Army?' And the poor lad gets all jittery.

Funny how we manage without men. The dockyard munitions plant had a football team, but what with the war there wasn't enough men to turn out. So girls filled in. Wouldn't surprise me if a few

74

of us turn out for Pompey one day. Some girls are really daring: wearing trousers, smoking, going to the flicks and pubs on their own, even wearing make-up and them do-dahs on their chest. They'll be wanting the vote next, I wouldn't wonder.

Now I don't want you to worry, but we've had a few scares round here lately. We thought the war wouldn't touch us. Well, it has. First two German aeroplanes flew over the town. Do you know what the cheeky monkeys did? They only went and dropped bricks on people's heads. Can you imagine? The papers say they've invented special darts that can split you in half from head to foot. How wicked!

It was quite good fun really. We all went out into the street to watch our gallant airmen from the Royal Flying Corps. They soon sent the horrid Hun packing with his tail between his legs. A bit scary though. To think you could be walking to work and the next thing you know you wake up dead.

Last Friday we had another nasty shock. I was on my way to school when someone says, 'Go back home, dearie, the Germans are coming.' Well, back indoors Mum was doing the washing when we thought we heard someone beating a carpet. Do you know what it was? A German battlecruiser had sailed up the Solent and was shelling the town.

What a cheek. It was mostly the dockyard that got a packet, but them bombs were close enough to blow out our windows and knock over the chimney. There were bits of shrapnel everywhere. One hit old Queenie Chapman up the street as she was getting her washing in. Gran put a hot bread poultice on her head and, when she took it off, there was a piece of shell the size of sixpence and as shiny as anything. Gran pulled it out with tweezers.

Do you remember the German family that ran the pork butchers round the corner? Well, the men got 'interned' two months ago, but after the shelling the rest of the family sent Queenie Chapman a bunch of flowers and a pork pie. Trust her. She wouldn't touch the pie cos she reckoned it was poisoned. So *we* ate it and it was delicious.

Do you know what puts the wind up people most? The telegram boy on his little red bike. Last Sunday, Mum, Doss, and I were getting dinner ready when the door goes—rat-tat-tat. It was him in his pillbox hat. I can see Mum now, all a-tremble, her hands floury and shaking like billy-o as she took the long buff thing. We thought it was you . . .

Luckily it was for the Garsides across the road. But they weren't home. It was their dad: killed in action.

At school Mr Cleal reads out the names of old boys who've been killed. And do you know, old Gingernob actually cries, the tears roll down his face. It amazes me and my chums cos we've never seen the Head cry before. Then we sing a hymn and have a minute's silence. I'm scared stiff he'll read out your name one morning. But *we* know you'll be safe.

Mrs Garside was comforted by a woman called Almira Brockway, a spiritualist or summat. This old gal said she'd spoken to Mrs Garside's dead hubbie, Fred, who had a message for her. He said to say how much he loved them all and was looking forward to them all being together in

Heaven. She charged Mrs Garside five bob for that message. Makes you wonder, don't it?

Well, dearest Jack, it's getting dark and I'm just about all in. So I'd better close now. I hope you like my cake. It's a bit burnt cos I left it too long in the oven. Sorry. Mum and Dad send love and kisses, as do all the kids. We miss you terribly. And we're proud of you (Mum says to add that bit).

Your ever-loving sis,

Floss

PS I must tell you something. I was walking home yesterday afternoon. There was a beautiful bright red sunset and, do you know what, it made the puddles on the road look like pools of blood. And all of a sudden I saw what *you* see over there. Write and tell me you're safe.

16

Jack shared the cake with his comrades-in-arms. Poor Harry hadn't received a thing, not a sausage. Freddie, though, had already got five letters from his mum—though he'd been chary about passing them round. 'They're a bit soppy,' he said. 'Mum still thinks I'm a baby.' But he was generous with his cakes and toffees. He kept the six pairs of socks and long johns for himself, since they were too baggy for the others.

That afternoon, filled with pictures of home, Jack squeezed into the trench 'funk hole' to pencil a reply. He had time on his hands till dusk, and a story or two to tell since he last wrote.

1 December 1914   'Over here'
Dear Floss and All,
    I'm not allowed to say where we are in case my letter falls into enemy hands and the Hun learns our whereabouts—even though he can see me fifty yards away. Daft I call it.
    Thanks a bunch for the smashing cake. It makes such a change to taste a bit of home cooking after our usual fare. The food here is mostly bully beef mixed with raw onions and a hunk of bread. Day in, day out. Now and again we get a treat: a tin of plum or apple jam. We use the tins for home-made bombs and the labels for bum paper.
    We were down to iron rations for a while—that's army biscuits as tough as old boots. You

78

can't sink your teeth into them. You just have to suck hard, like on gobstoppers. Some lads use them as picture frames, sticking a girlfriend's photo in, with a bit of boot black round the edges for show.

We're so lucky to have some bright sparks up at Company HQ to look after us. A week ago the order came down: 'Keep the men on iron rations to toughen them up.' Well, stap me. We'd give our back teeth for a nice drop of bacon fat to dunk our bread in. It's fine and dandy for them, what with their weekly hamper from Harrods. So what did we do?

We stuck a notice up saying, 'No hot rations. No blooming War!'

Next day we're back on hot rations double quick.

Even better. Jerry must have got wind of our notice because he tossed us over some sausage and tins of pork!

We often have a good old chinwag across No Man's Land, calling out 'Comrade' or 'Kamerad', or 'Tommy' or 'Fritz'. You get a few German lads who speak some English. The other night they asked us if we'd lost a corporal called William Cooper. The poor soul had got caught in gunfire on a prisoner-grabbing mission. Someone yelled back 'Yes,' and a German voice said not to worry, they'd given him a decent send-off.

'Thanks, Fritzie,' yelled one of our men. 'Aren't you sick of it all?' And he got the answer, 'Yes, aren't you?'

Another fellow shouted, 'Wouldn't you like peace?' to which the reply was, 'Yes, yes, let's have it now.'

They're just like us really, fighting someone else's war, eager to get back to civvy street. I bet right now one of them's writing home to his little sister, just like me.

A lot of our lads are browned off. We haven't been relieved for sixteen days. We're covered in slime and often have to fling ourselves flat on our faces in the thick mud. I haven't washed for ages, my beard is as long as the King's and I'm itchy all over. Not a pretty sight or smell, I can tell you.

Our company is down to about sixty—from over two hundred. Some idiot gives the order to attack, uphill, right under the noses of German machine-gunners in their concrete pillboxes. It's damn suicide. Attack and counter-attack. One step forward, two steps back.

The strain is taking its toll. Nerves are getting frayed. The other day there was a chappie lying next to me with his legs in the air. I says, 'Keep your pins down.' 'Why?' he says. 'You'll get shot,' I says. 'But I want a little blighty in the leg, so's I can go home,' he says. 'I don't fancy one in the guts.'

Some blokes even whisper the word 'prisoner' as if that's the answer. Anything's better than this! Let me read from my diary.

Monday 25 November

8 p.m. Expecting an attack at any moment. Talk of recapturing the trenches with bayonets. Where are the officers? None around. Left to ourselves. No sleep, no water, impossible to move out of the hole, even show heads above trench. Afternoon and evening dreadful, inferno of fire. Surrounded by corpses—disgusting smell.

10 p.m. Big commotion, red and white flares, chatter of machine guns, thunder of artillery, 400

yards away. Enemy getting ready. Every man at his post waiting, whole night through. Will Boche rush us from top of ridge? Shells explode only feet away, all around men fall wounded. Blinded by shells and earth thrown up. Men slip off duckboards into churned-up mud, sucked down forever.

Tuesday 26 November

Impossible to get any kip, deluge of shells continues through night. Frantic orders 'You may be attacked, be ready!' We've been ready three days and nights. Shells, shrapnel falling like hail non-stop. Everything trembling, nerves and ground. Near end of tether. Crouch down, packs on backs, waiting, scanning top of ridge. Lasts till nightfall. Dazed, hungry, feverish, thirsty. No water. Have to drink. Take a chance and drink from shell hole. Wet mouth from water running red with blood.

At 9 p.m. avalanche of fire burst on ridge. An attack?

At 11 p.m. we're off, over the top. At last! Land swept constantly with machine-gun fire and flares. Every ten steps fall flat to ground so as not to be seen. Ground littered with corpses. Stumble forward, falling into shell holes, walking over dead bodies, flinging myself flat, face in someone's dead guts.

Glimpse of hell.

Wednesday 27 November

At 3 a.m. our troops attack us from behind, trying to recapture ground lost day before. Fall on us, thinking they've found the Boche. Our 75s fire at us! Bloody idiots. Terrific panic. Six wounded at one go from shell burst. Want to run for it. Don't know what to do. Blood flows, corpses stink, flies buzz. Enough to drive you mad. Two men top themselves.

6 a.m. Now Boche begin to pound our positions. Shells from front and rear, ours and theirs. Sure Boche preparing attack. Shells scream down on every side. At 6.30, dazed and numb, firing range lengthens and suddenly everyone on feet, shouting, 'Boche coming. Boche coming!'

They attack in formation, columns of eight. Our troops at posts in flash. Hold our fire until Boche ten yards away, then let them have it. Guns bark, machine gun opens up.

Boche cut down. Amid smoke, see scores of dead and wounded, some calling for mercy: 'Comrade, don't shoot. I surrender.'

Take no prisoners.

Germans retreating to trenches.

CO of force behind us suddenly realizes mistake. Stops shelling us, sends runner to say reinforcements on way—when we don't need them. Still, handy for supplies and carting off wounded.

Only around 9 a.m. gets quieter. Help wounded. Some past it. Tommies and Fritzes stuck on barbed wire as in spider's web. Our shell holes are lakes of mud. Raining, rifles don't work. If they come again have to rely on bayonets.

By evening still no relief. Another twenty-four hours to get through. Gets colder at night, lie down in mud and wait.

Thursday 28 November

Attacks and counter-attacks. Toughest day yet. Shelling and tiredness harder to take. At 10 a.m. Boche pound us with all they've got. Head's buzzing, had enough. Me, Harry, and Freddie squashed in hole, protecting ourselves from bullets and shrapnel with packs. Await shell to end it all.

Please God it comes soon.

All at once, firing ends. Silence. Nothing happens. Look at one another, trembling all over, half crazy. Will it start over again?

At last, we're relieved. Cry of joy from those left alive. Tiredness melts away, limbs regain enough strength to escape to safety.

Halt, guns rumbling in distance, able to breathe at last. Sarge calls the roll.

How many men missing when names called!

That's war, Sis. That's what it's like. Some say we're lucky to be alive. Yes, it's luck all right. Living—if that's the word—among the dead and dying, amid unimaginable hardships and heartaches.

Yes, we're glad to be alive, glad only for you at home.

If you could look into our eyes you'd see the horror of it all.

I can't write any more.
Give my love to everyone.

Your loving brother,
Jack

17

6 December 1914

Dear Floss,

I feel mad at myself for that last letter. I was
dog tired, as bitter as lemons. Sorry, Sis. I've had
a chance to perk up behind the lines, brush the
cobwebs out of my brain, disinfect my body of lice
and lies. What *is* truth in war?

It's not what you're told. It's what you see with
your own two eyes. There's another truth the eyes
sometimes see. Let me tell you about it.

At night on sentry duty, I sometimes think I'm
the only man in the world. It's so quiet. Soldiers
are sleeping. Theirs and ours. I look up at the
stars, as bright as tin pans in the dark sky,
scrubbed and hung out to dry. They look so alive,
twinkling and winking down at me. No wonder
they've been the friend and guide of seafarers
down the ages.

I try to remember their names. Those two
holding hands are Gemini, the Twins; there's
grumpy old Mother Bear with Little Bear; fierce
Taurus the Bull about to charge; Cancer the Crab,
scrabbling sideways towards the Moon. And the
brightest of all, Morning Star, lighting our way.
When I get home I'll buy a telescope and study the
stars.

Of a daytime I watch the white clouds drift
lazily over the battlefield, I listen to the larks and
thrushes singing. The birds don't stop and say,

'Oh, pardon me for disturbing you, there's a war on, I'd better not sing here.' No, they sing their little hearts out for us, Tommy and Fritz alike. They don't take sides.

All around, men are dying and you can't help noticing the contrast between what we've done to nature and how nature goes on its own sweet way. Whatever we do, whatever we destroy, seeds are still growing in their beds, bulbs come out and flowers bloom. Stars, birds, flowers . . . especially daisies, they're scattered everywhere.

You see a bank of late daisies half as wide as a street, yellow and white and pink. They even grow in clusters along the top of the trench.

An officer came along the other day and gave me a cup to fit on my rifle; it's to fire a rifle grenade. When he'd gone I picked a bunch of daisies and put them in the cup with some water. What a lovely fresh smell. It took me back to lying on the grass in summer meadows.

I shed a tear or two. Funny that: dead comrades, no, yet daisies made me cry.

I was chatting to an Indian sepoy yesterday, and we got round to the beauty of nature. Here he is, five thousand miles from the warm sun of India, stuck in this dismal sea of mud and snow (it's started snowing). No warm clothing, no officer to speak his lingo, living on half our pay and rations. And he talked of nature, of the mango trees and purple rhododendron bushes in his garden, of sunbaked plains and sunrise on the Ganges.

When I asked him what he was doing so far from home, he told an amazing story. The British

Viceroy had told India it too was at war since it was part of our Empire. So men were rounded up and sent to fight for a freedom they were denied themselves. Mind you, the Viceroy promised that if they helped set Europe free, the British King would set them free.

I got the feeling that my Indian mate didn't trust our promises.

We may have had it rough, but, by Heaven, those poor sods always get pitched into the heaviest fighting. If there's ever a suicide charge to be made, the Indian Corps is sent in. Three weeks ago, they were sent to capture trenches no one else could take. Jerry must have had quite a shock seeing hordes of dark-skinned men in turbans come rushing at him, yelling and shrieking. He upped and ran, and we retook the trenches.

I've never seen such brave fellows. It's earned them half a dozen Victoria Crosses. Naturally, they all went to their British officers. 'Tut-tut, can't give old Vickie to the natives, can you!'

War can bring out the worst as well as the best in people. I was in a party of men sent to collect up stray guns and we came upon a heap of dead bodies—nine of them hit by one shell. They were all funny shapes. As I glanced round, I saw some geezer taking a wristwatch off a dead body. I couldn't help myself: I told him to put it down. The surly codger did, but he didn't like it.

When you pass dead bodies, the pockets are almost always hanging out. I've come across men with six watches taken off dead officers, three on each wrist. There are two London lads who've been looting graves, getting gold rings off corpses. That's nasty. It doesn't matter whether the bodies are ours or theirs, you should show some respect. We had a copper in our platoon. He got shot up the backside and was bleeding badly. While he was waiting for a stretcher he kept mumbling and pointing down the line. It turned out he'd been collecting best quality German cut-throat razors. He was desperate not to leave them behind.

War can make people very selfish.

Christmas is coming, the goose is getting fat . . . I don't think I fancy roast goose this year. I've asked Father Christmas to bring me a leg of ham, sucking pig, and plum duff. Sarge reckons we'll be lucky to get a tin of bully beef.

To think how Ginger Cleal assured us we'd all be home by Christmas. 'Mustn't miss the fun,' he said. Not a cat's chance in hell. Jerry and us, we're still doing our 'Here we go round the mulberry bush' lark. 'Atishoo, Atishoo, we all fall down.' Except some stay down and others carry on dancing till finally we all fall down.

Oh dear, there I go again, bellyaching. Sorry.

So far, so good, we're surviving. Not a scratch.

I'm glad to hear you girls are sticking up for yourselves. If you carry on like that you'll be leading armies one day. You couldn't make a worse job of it than our generals. Mind you, you'd probably spoil the fun by ending all wars and putting them out of their cushy jobs. Hurry up and take over so's we can come home.

Harry says to ask his mum to write—he hasn't had a word from home yet. And please thank Freddie's mum for sending the socks she knitted.

That's all, my big-little, brave-little sister. I love you all. Write soon. Your letters mean so much.

Your ever loving brother,

Jack

x x x x x x x

PS Don't forget to feed my rabbits—they like dandelion and dock leaves and lamb's tails best. Give them clean straw once a week. Ta ever so.

18

While shepherds watched their flocks by night
  All seated on the ground,
A high-explosive shell came down
  And mutton rained around.

Saki

After ten days on Easy Street it was back to the Front.

While Jack's platoon was resting behind the lines, a company of new recruits arrived. It was easy to tell the old and new apart: by the eyes. The new—all wide and bright and innocent. Jack suddenly saw how much he'd aged; each frontline day had added a year. Looking at the raw youths he saw himself as he was a lifetime ago.

War does that. It turns your skin a murky yellow, like a well-used cricket bat; it gives you a world-weary, hard-baked look. But, above all, war is in the eyes. Look closely and you'll see there pictures of all the suffering and pain, all the horrors the eyes have seen.

Off they went, brand new and soiled, on a bitterly cold morning in mid-December. It was a four-mile march—or, rather, slip, slide, stumble, and fall over frosty churned-up earth.

The men they were replacing were cheery Yorkshire tykes who said how quiet it had been.

'Nowt for days,' one remarked. 'Just the odd shell to tell us Jerry's still about.'

The troops made quite a din as they filtered up the line, with guns and limbers further back rattling their steel

89

wheels on the rutted roads. Some of the new boys burst into song:

> 'It's a long way to Tipperary
> It's a long way to go.
> It's a long way to Tipperary
> To the sweetest girl I know.'

Let them sing, thought Jack, while they've still a voice to sing with.

The Germans must have heard the racket and thought an attack was in the offing. No sooner had the new troops settled in the trenches than:

BIFF! BANG! WALLOP!

Jerry started blasting them with all he'd got. High explosive shells came raining down and blowing the trenches to pieces. The noise was unbearable. All Jack and his mates could do was get their heads down and wait for a break, or for English guns to open up. It might be hours.

All at once, Jack noticed one of the new lads standing up. He was shaking jerkily, like a wound-up metal toy. He must have gone barmy, for he was screeching, 'Bugger this! I can't stand it any more!'

Next thing Jack knew, he was climbing from the trench with his bayonet at the ready. He said he was going to do Jerry and stick cold steel up him.

'If anyone tries to stop me, they'll get my bayonet.'

What could they do? They let him go.

God knows what happened. Just rat-tat-tat.

He didn't come back.

Shortly after that shelling ceased. The silence was as deafening as a shell-burst. Jack and Harry stood up to survey the damage.

'Come on, Freddie,' called Harry. 'Don't lie there all day hoping for a blighty.'

A low gurgle from Freddie's throat made Jack and Harry whip round in alarm. Freddie was lying on his back with both legs in the air. His right foot had gone. Shrapnel had evidently caught him behind the heel and taken the sole clean off. It left his big toe spinning round and round on a bit of gristle. When the medical orderly came up, he casually snipped the toe off and tossed it over the top.

Poor Freddie was blubbering like a baby. His mates did their best to comfort him while waiting for the stretcher.

'You lucky bleeder,' said Harry. 'Got yourself a nice little blighty; they'll whisk you home in time for Christmas. No more soldiering for you.'

'Will they cut my foot off?' whined Freddie through his tears.

'Nah,' said Jack. 'It's only a nick. You never did like football anyhow.'

Jack and Harry glanced at one another unsurely. Was Freddie lucky to be out of it? Was the loss of a foot a price worth paying? One thing's for certain: he wouldn't be needing all those pairs of socks his mum had knitted.

'See you back home, chum,' they called as two orderlies stretchered him off. Freddie didn't reply.

Jerry opened up again soon after, this time scoring a direct hit on the ammo store. The first sounds the soldiers heard didn't give fair warning of what was to follow—just a series of fire crackers: pop-pop-pop-pop!

That was just the prelude to one God-Almighty B-A-N-G!!!

Anyone within twenty-five yards would have had their eardrums blasted through their head, passing each other in the middle. But that wasn't all.

The exploding bullets and shells set the whole caboodle alight at the back of Jack's trench. The only way out for the flying hungry flames was sideways, down the length of the dug-out. The orangey-purple billows swept up soldiers in their paths like a raging bush fire does dry twigs.

The poor bleeders didn't stand an earthly.

Above the furnace roar screamed an order:

'Abandon post!'

Harry made it. Jack didn't.

Both were lucky enough to be at one end of the trench, out of range of the flames, if not the heat. The trouble was they had to run *towards* the exploding store to escape to safety; steps led down to the rear dug-out. Anyone popping their head over the parapet was likely to get it blown off.

Jack would have got out but for a bit of bad luck. As he rushed towards the steps, someone made a grab at him with one fiery hand. The man was enveloped in a rolling ball of fire.

There was nothing Jack could do, either to help him or to break free. If he stayed there a moment longer he'd be fried to a frazzle.

'Sorry, mate,' he muttered.

He punched the man full in his melting face.

As the man slumped to the trench floor, Jack stumbled on. But it was too late: he'd copped a searing blast of red-hot fire on the side of his head.

His brown hair went up in smoke and the pain in his eyes became so unbearable that he wanted to claw them out. He couldn't open his eyes at all: the swollen eyelids seemed stuck together with strong gum.

As he groped his way along the trench, he felt himself walking over dead bodies mixed up with piles of soft earth; it was so slippery he kept falling over. Finally, someone gave him a shoulder to hang on to, and he was led down steps into the escape trench.

After a while, he climbed thankfully into the fresh air and was told to join a line of other fire-blinded men. They then had to walk three or four miles to a first-aid post, the blind leading the blind, left hand on left shoulder of the man in front. It must have looked like a giant caterpillar crawling across the rutted land.

Once at base camp, they were sorted out into 'Badly' and 'Less Badly' burned, and those 'Playing Up'. Jack made the middle group.

He was put on a stretcher waiting to be taken down the line for treatment. All they did here was sorting out and patching up. As he lay on the floor of what smelt like an old flour mill, he thought grimly of Army fire advice:

'Pee into handkerchief. Tie round nose and mouth.'

But what if you don't want a wee? Or if you can't find your red-spotted handkerchief?

All around him men were crying out in pain, not so much from smarting eyes, but from flesh burnt by the flames. One man said it was like having scalding water poured over your skin. Although Jack was blind and had singed lungs, he could thank his lucky stars he had no serious skin burns: the flames burned right through your body and out the other side.

After an orderly had bathed his eyes and covered them with a wad of lint, he was taken by truck to the nearest army hospital. It was a bumpy journey that gave him time to reflect on events.

How was Harry doing without him? It was the first time they'd been apart.

Were his burns bad enough for a trip home?

Could he be home for Christmas?

He'd have to write to his family before they got the official notice: 'We regret to inform you that your son has been wounded on active service . . . '

That would give them forty fits, wondering if he'd lost arms and legs.

He was out of luck. All his wound earned was a week's

'convalescence'. His sight returned in a day or so and he was able to walk about the hospital and its grounds. It was while he was wandering through a ward that he heard his name being called.

'Jack. Jack, is that you?'

As he glanced round in surprise, who should he see but Freddie, propped up against a pillow in an iron bed. Funny, he'd clean forgotten about Freddie and his foot. Jack's gaze automatically shifted to the patient's feet beneath the sheet.

His face muscles tightened. He saw the outline of only one leg!

'They've amputated my leg,' said Freddie.

Jack didn't know what to say. He'd guessed the foot would go, just below the ankle. *But not the whole leg*. It must've been more serious than he'd thought.

'So you'll be going home a war hero, Freddie.'

Freddie stared hopefully at his friend.

'Do you really think so?'

''Course, soon as you're well enough.'

Freddie eased himself up on one elbow, crooked a finger and beckoned Jack within whispering range.

'I don't think I'll make it.'

'Codswallop, matey. Having a leg off's no big deal. These days they've got wonderful artificial limbs. No one'll notice under your trouser leg, once you get used—'

'I've got gangrene,' Freddie said quietly. 'It's eating away at me, creeping into my guts.'

Jack was shocked. He didn't know what to say. In the end, he just mumbled, 'Is that what the *doctor* says?'

'He said they'd found a spot of gangrene. I know it's worse than that.'

He shook his head miserably and began to cry.

Jack wanted to say that 'a spot' of gangrene didn't mean curtains, they could cut it out, like the maggoty bit from an apple. But he kept quiet, his mouth working at the corners, unable to find the right words.

Freddie lay still for a while, eyelids wet and closed. Then, without opening his eyes, he murmured, 'You and Harry can have my socks and long johns.'

Jack bit his tongue. If Freddie opened his eyes, he couldn't fail to notice the horror on Jack's face as he looked closer at his friend.

Freddie's lips were dry and purple; the top teeth stuck out over the thin bottom lip; a hank of dark hair flopped forward over the damp, chalky-white brow; the eyes had shrunk back inside dark rings.

Jack's head was throbbing, his eyes felt as if someone was stabbing them with sharp pins, and the smell of gangrene mixed with carbolic was irritating his lungs. It was getting dark. He had to get away.

'I'll be back early tomorrow, Freddie. Get some sleep, old son. You'll pull through.'

With that feeble farewell, Jack hurried from the ward and made his way through the french doors into the garden. The hospital must have once been a fancy chateau, for the gardens stretched as far as the eye could see, with statues and busts and sculptured bushes. Despite the cold, he sank down on a green bench and put his head in his hands.

Poor old Freddie. He thought of the stout woman with tears streaming down her cheeks as she'd begged him to look after her son. What was he to say to her? Maybe Freddie would recover, they'd go down the pub for a Brickies and laugh about it all . . .

A sharp noise made him jump. The wind must have slammed a door to. Medical orderlies were dashing in and out of the building. Jack heard a shout, 'The bloody fool's put a bullet through his brain.'

19

Jack was still sitting on the bench, cold and numb, when an orderly came for him.

'You a mate of Frederick George Feltham, 15th Hants?'

He gave the man a dazed look; his brain raced madly over the stops.

Surely not! No, no, not our Freddie, he wouldn't do a thing like that. Tell me it's not him . . .

He finally found his voice.

' 'Sright.'

'Follow me.'

He got unsteadily to his feet and tagged on behind, hoping against hope the man would turn left, away from Freddie's ward. No, a right turn, third bed on the left. Freddie's bed.

He is dead.

His face is still wet with tears. His eyes are half open, their big brown pupils as dull as stewed prunes.

They'd had time to clean him up. The bullet had gone clean through his mouth and out the back of his head. Jack stared down at the corpse, but not for long. He couldn't bear it. There it was, with its face now set, pale and still oozing blood, when only an hour ago they'd sat together, chatting, planning the future . . .

Jack surprised himself. Now that he was faced with death, he was remarkably calm. He wasn't sickened by the

96

sight of dark red blood on pasty yellow skin. Perhaps he'd become so accustomed to death that, instead of feeling sorry for Freddie, he could look on his death with no more than a shrug.

After all, he himself might die at any moment; a friend could be looking down at him.

Pity was with the angels.

The orderly roused him from his thoughts.

'You takin' 'is fings?'

Jack nodded.

'We need the bed, see. Poor beggars are lying on the corridor floor freezing their bollocks off.'

Jack undid the identity tag from round Freddie's neck and picked up his bag. Then he turned and walked away, his feet moving his boots forward.

He was still in a daze when he returned to the garden bench: the darkness and cool breeze were a relief. He set his face into the wind and took a deep gulp of chill air. The sudden draught seared his damaged lungs, making him cough and wheeze and hug his aching chest.

When he'd recovered, he sat back, his eyes screwed tight, taking half breaths, filtering the hostile air through teeth and tongue. Pictures of school desks, rounders, hymn singing, hop scotch, marbles in the gutter . . . and Freddie's dumpy mother, all flapped wildly through his mind, like a caged bird trying to escape.

One of Ginger Cleal's boys gone. Two to go. Worth a word at morning assembly?

As he sat there in the quiet of evening, he suddenly heard singing from an upstairs window. For a moment, he thought he was back at school.

It was a single, beautiful voice, ringing out into the night.

> All things bright and beautiful,
> All creatures great and small,
> All things wise and wonderful,
> The Lord God loves them all.

The dark forms of trees loomed above him like shadows of giants, and in the night sky the stars stood so bright and close it seemed he could reach up and touch them. What with the singing and the shadows, he felt so uplifted, above earthly cares, he could almost fly away, floating up and down among the stars.

For some reason he said a prayer for Freddie, under his breath.

When Jack returned to the 'Eye, Nose, and Throat' ward, he sat on the edge of his bed and wrote a letter. The words didn't come easy.

Dear Mrs Feltham,

   You will know by now that Freddie is no more.

   You asked me to look after your son. Sadly, I failed.

   I can only say that with a soldier as brave as your son, even his Guardian Angel could not protect him. He was always loyal to his comrades and a daring soldier.

   Freddie was always talking about you, how fond he was of his family, how much he loved you all.

   The Army will send you his effects.

   Freddie died a hero's death, on the battlefield. Truly, he died that others might live. You can be very proud of him.

   I am honoured to have been your son's friend.

                    I remain, yours sincerely
                         Private Jack Loveless

Jack signed the letter and read it through, cursing the words that were so stiff and awkward . . . and false. Why couldn't he tell the truth?

Freddie shot himself because of this horrid, bloody useless war.

He didn't want to be a hero. He just wanted to be a Man—despite his mother.

Suicide is better than rotting away with stinking gangrene. It takes a Real Man to shoot himself.

After slipping his letter into the green envelope, and ticking the box that confirmed he hadn't given away secrets, Jack rummaged through Freddie's things. He took out the grey woolly socks, unused long johns, and a half-eaten packet of Huntley and Palmer biscuits. The rest could be sent home.

That night he had a nightmare about being blown to bits—all they could identify him by were torn-off legs clothed in grey socks and baggy long johns. Freddie ended up getting two graves and Jack none. He became The Unknown Soldier.

A few days later he was discharged from hospital. Along with a few dozen other walking wounded, he was herded into the back of a truck and driven to the Front.

'Patch 'em up and chuck 'em back. And don't return alive!' as the orderly said, only half joking.

He went back to his regiment, taking his place in the trenches beside Harry.

'You still alive?' was the cheery greeting.

'I might ask the same of you!' retorted Jack with a grin as they punched each other's shoulder with genuine joy.

'Here, I've brought you a present: Freddie's last request—two pairs of socks, brand new, one pair of long johns, never worn, and six bickies, uneaten.'

Jack told Harry the news.

'Poor old Tubs,' said Harry with a sigh. 'By the way, fair exchange is no robbery. Here's something for you.'

Jack's eyes lit up as he saw the envelope. As always when he received something as personal as a letter from home, he had an overwhelming urge to be alone. It was too private to share with others, in the trenches. The nearest any soldier came to privacy was the latrines—if that was not too grand a name for the shit hole and squat pole across it.

Nonetheless, Jack took his letter to the lav. Before opening it, he sniffed it all over, filling his nose with imaginary smells of home, then lit a fag to block out the stink rising from below.

10 December 1914
Dear Jack,
   I don't have much time cos I'm tidy busy, what with the kids (Mum's gone down with a gippy tum) and my part-time job. So you'll have to excuse this letter being short.
   The big news is that Dad's joined up. I don't think you'll bump into him as he's gone somewhere called Alexandria—it's in North Africa, Dad says, by the Pyramids.
   One thing more. On Sunday, me and Hilda Perham cycled up to Fort Purbrook on the Hill. They've turned it into a prisoner-of-war camp, full of creepy-crawly Germans. I was curious to see what sort of beasts they are, those nasty men who are trying to kill my brave brother. They turned out to be so manky I almost felt sorry for them.
   One bloke spoke some English and said how pleased he was to get captured and come to England—because he could have some decent

grub. He said he'd had to live on mangel-wurzels: turnip soup for breakfast, turnip jam on turnip bread for dinner, and turnip mash for tea washed down with acorn coffee. He was so starved he ate the yard-dog's stone-hard biscuits.

I don't think you've much to fear from scarecrows like him.

That's all my news. Be careful, Jack. We all send our love. When next I write I'll send Dad's address in the Pyramids.

Your loving sister,
Floss

PS   Oh yes, and Mrs Feltham says please to look after Freddie.

Oh, and another thing: if I don't write before, Merry Christmas.

Well, I'm blowed, thought Jack as he returned to the trenches. It's Christmas Eve!

20

You talk o' better food for us, an' schools, an' fires,
  an' all:
We'll wait for extra rations if you treat us rational.
Don't mess about the cook-room slops, but prove it to
  our face
The Widow's Uniform is not the soldier-man's
  disgrace.
For it's Tommy this, an' Tommy that, an' 'Chuck
  him out, the brute!'
But it's 'Saviour of 'is country' when the guns begin
  to shoot;
An' it's Tommy this, an' Tommy that, an' anything
  you please;
An' Tommy ain't a bloomin' fool—you bet that
  Tommy sees!

from 'Tommy' by Rudyard Kipling

It was snowing.

'Looks like a white Christmas,' remarked Harry.

Jack watchfully peered out onto No Man's Land.

A snowy white sheet covered the naked body of earth between the trenches. No Man's Land was dead right: no man dared cross it. Those that did lay stiff and torn like twisted thorn trees.

It was a football pitch wide, full of frosty water holes, barbed wire glinting in the sun, and crumpled silvery grey-brown bundles lying either side of the halfway line.

'Quiet, ain't it?' said Jack. 'Real Christmassy. I think I'll ask Sarge if I can pop down to Company Headquarters with Freddie's things. It'll be nice to get shot of 'em before Christmas. I should be back in an hour or so.'

Harry snorted. 'I'll ask Jerry to hold fire till you get back.'

Grudgingly, Sergeant Hickey let Jack fall out.

'And no dawdling. Be back here by fifteen hundred hours or I'll be handing in *your* effects, got it!'

'What if they invite me to dinner, Sarge?'

'Yeah, and pigs'll fly! Git aht of it!'

Jack zigzagged down the trench maze with Freddie's bag over one shoulder, his rifle over the other. Snow muffled his bootsteps, drawing a veil over the mud and filth. As he trotted along, his thoughts were of the folks at home on Christmas Day: sitting round the Christmas Tree—eating one of his rabbits for dinner!—drinking a cup of Mum's home-made damson cordial.

'Here's to Dad.'

'Here's to our Jack.'

'Merry Christmas, one and all.'

With a sigh of relief, Jack spotted the Company HQ in the distance. He had visions of getting lost and stumbling into a German trench. 'Oh, just dropped in for Christmas grog!' What a nice Christmas present that'd be!

The HQ and Officers' Mess was an old farm cottage nestling in a dell of poplars. It even had its own chickens and a herd of three or four Jersey cows—keeping the officers in the manner to which they were accustomed: fresh eggs and fresh milk for breakfast.

As he drew close he noticed men in an orchard behind the cottage. Two senior officers with red tabs, all spick and span, were standing to one side, leaning on their shooting sticks and cheering 'rah-rah-rah'.

The spectacle they were watching was most extraordinary.

Two bare-headed fellows in shirt and braces were

duelling, armed with long sticks stuck with apples, while four others were pelting each other with rotten fruit and snowballs.

They were having a jolly old time, judging from the whoops and shouts:

'Got you, you rotter!'

'Missed me, boo-hoo!'

'You're a frightful shot.'

'What ripping fun.'

Jack was treated as if he was just another rotten plum. He half expected them to come chasing after him as their quarry for pigsticking.

It's the closest these beggars'll come to war, he thought bitterly.

He couldn't help comparing their stick-fight fun with bayoneting and machine-gunning every day on the battlefield.

After standing around for ten minutes, waiting to be summoned—'Speak only when spoken to!' Captain Cleal had told him about officers—Jack turned towards the cottage back door. In white paint someone had neatly written 'GARRICK CLUB' across the rough wood.

He knocked politely.

'Come,' came a cheery chorus.

Pushing open the door, he stepped smartly inside and saluted.

Sitting round an oak table covered with a blue and white check tablecloth was a group of seven officers. From their faces he could tell they hadn't expected *him* to disturb their lunch.

'Yes?'

'I've brought my dead friend's effects, sir.'

'Yes?'

'To send home, sir.'

'Yes?'

104

'That's all, sir.'

'Wait.'

The gentlemen turned back to their lunch.

In or out? Now that he was inside, Jack was going to stay put, in the warm. He put down his rifle and pack, and stood at ease in the corner, hands behind his back, twiddling his thumbs. After a while he began to get anxious. Sarge wanted him back by three.

All he needed was to hand over the bag and have it signed for. That wouldn't take two ticks. But no, lunch came first. War could wait. What bounders those Boche were to disturb the peace and quiet with their nasty faraway shelling.

What did Jack have in common with these men?

He stared at them, searching for a similarity in face or gesture, language or clothes. And he came to the conclusion that they were nothing but stuck-up, toffee-nosed bullies. Whose side were they on? Their own, of course. Theirs was a different war: all strutting and breast-beating, power and glory. War was a game played on the sports fields of their public schools.

There are three sides to this war, decided Jack: them, us, and the Germans.

The smell of food was making his belly rumble. The seven officers, white bibs tucked into shirts like dribbling infants, were chewing on beefsteaks, peas, and fried potatoes. They washed it all down with bottles of claret— no doubt filched from the farmer's cellar. Then they chucked tinned fruit and cheese down their gobs. It was the cheese that excited the liveliest debate.

'Good cheeses of the small Dutch variety are top-hole.'

'I prefer a spot of Stilton, on rye bread. Can't beat it, don't you know.'

'The Mess President has just taken delivery of a spiffing hamper of Brie and Camembert. Delightful pong.'

'Pity the port's run out.'

Jack couldn't wait to get his teeth into a hard tack biscuit washed down with petrol-perfumed water.

After thanking God for what they'd just received, the company chaplain got up to relieve Jack of his precious burden.

'Paybook?'

Jack looked nonplussed.

'Dunno, sir. Still at the hospital I guess.'

'Nincompoop! How can these rags get home with no address?'

'I'll write it down, sir.'

'Oh, so you can write, can you?'

He glanced round with a smirk at his pals. This was the after-lunch entertainment: a bit of knock-about music-hall stuff.

'You could be stealing his worldly goods, for all I know. I've met your type before.'

Jack took that as a 'Yes'.

He took a pencil from his pocket, licked the lead, and carefully printed on the back of Freddie's bag:

> Private F. Feltham, 0176392
> 21 Carnarvon Road
> Copnor
> Portsmouth
> Hampshire

'Dismiss.'

He couldn't get back to the line quick enough. So much for 'God rest you, merry gentlemen'! But what about the privates, corporals, and sergeants? The parson's nose for them.

He blew a raspberry.

'Freddie, old son,' muttered Jack with a glance upwards, 'if you're looking down, I hope you appreciate this.'

On the way back, Jack thought about officers. For the first time war had brought upper and lower classes together. At home they were total strangers. They lived separate lives—in state or private school, in town or country house, in factory or office, mine or cloister.

Now, in war, all soldiers were equal before the gun. Men were stripped of the figleaf of birth; they were judged solely on how they acted under fire. Many officers failed the test and were exposed to public gaze, like the Emperor with no clothes. What they feared most of all was that, after the war, the men who'd fought for freedom in France and Belgium might demand it at home, sweeping away their wealth and privilege.

To be fair, Jack had come across a few decent sorts who'd mucked in with the men. He remembered one, a shy quiet type, a poet—Lieutenant Charles Middleton. Only twenty he was. Very la-di-da. Despite his Scottish background he spoke that strange brand of King's English that tied together all public schoolboys, like a sack of rotting plums.

Charles Middleton wanted to get close to his men, but found it hard to break down barriers. Yet when he read out a couple of his poems he hit the button, expressed men's feelings better than they could themselves.

Charlie Middleton was as brave—or foolhardy—as he was bitter. Not for him leading from behind. He was always first out of the trenches. Once he led a company into attack against the first line of German trenches. So fierce was his charge that the men took the trenches and held on to them . . . until the Hun used their 'wonder weapon'—the machine gun.

Heavens Above! That mowed them down all right. Few of Charlie Middleton's men escaped alive; the unlucky ones that did were dragged out full of holes and bleeding red. No one ever found young Charlie's body.

21

It was the clearest, most beautiful night of the old year, as still and pure as Christmas ought to be. It was freezing, too, which put the seal on squelchy mud. Men's thoughts were far from mud and guns and killing. It was Christmas Eve.

All at once, about nine o'clock, a most peculiar sound drifted on the wind across the sleeping divide. It was coming from the German trenches—a sort of buzzing, sighing, humming noise like a swarm of honey bees.

With an anxious frown, Harry turned to Jack.

'Aye-aye, what's Jerry up to now?'

'Could be his secret weapon—buzzing bluebottles.'

'Hold hard, matey; sounds like a bit of a sing-song.'

They both strained their ears.

As the wind rose, odd sounds floated over the battlefield. Mouth organ, accordion, snatches of song.

''Snice,' said Harry. 'Reminds me of Crystal Palace, fans singing before the Final.'

The song rose and dipped like a soaring swallow.

'''Silent Night'', ain't it?'

'Well, I'm blessed. So it is. Cheeky blighters. Fancy pinching one of our carols. Here, let's give them one back. How about ''Once in Royal David's City''?'

Jack and Harry raised their voices, dum-dum-dumming to forgotten lines. Other English throats took up the tune, plugging the gaps, stoking the fire of song until music filled the frosty air.

When they ran out of words there was a moment's lull before clapping came from the German side, and shouts of, 'Bravo, Tommy!'

Not to be outdone, back bounced the Germans. First a mouth organ played a verse before voices joined in with 'O, Come All Ye Faithful'. The English heard it through and gave a round of applause.

'Very nice, Fritz!'

'Come on, boyos, we can do better than that,' yelled Staff Sergeant 'Taff' Morris down the line. 'Let's teach them to sing ''Silent Night'' properly.'

He'd grown up in the South Wales coalfields, singing in a chapel choir; he had a strong baritone voice that rang out like a tuneful foghorn through the still, silent night.

'Silent Night, Holy Night,
All is calm, all is bright . . . '

Before he got any further English and German voices took up the song. And the two choirs, friend and foe, sang in harmony. First sweet and low, then surging up to the rafters of the skies.

It was as if an invisible choirmaster was conducting a heavenly choir. Was there ever a more moving carol sung?

In the hush that followed, no man dared break the magic spell. For a couple of minutes. Deathly silence.

Then, all at once, a lone German voice rang out:

'Hey, Tommy, Merry Christmas.'

'And to you, Fritz,' shouted 'Taff' Morris.

On both sides, voices took up the cry:

'Happy Christmas.'

'Fröhliche Weihnachten!'

Then loud cheering and clapping. No Man's Land resounded with friendship and goodwill—to all men, Tommy and Fritz alike.

Through the dark, a voice suddenly cut through the greetings.

'Hey, Englisher, what about a Christmas truce? No more shooting, *ja*?'

For a while the English trenches fell silent. Since all the senior officers had sloped off to Christmas service, there was no experienced officer in command. Evidently their Christian brothers over the way had done the same.

'Right,' sang out a loud baritone voice. 'I'll take charge. Be it on my head.'

It was Staff Sergeant Morris.

'OK, boys?' he shouted down the line.

The roar that met his shout contained all the pent-up feelings of the men. It was the most democratic decision of the war. The soldiers had made themselves heard above the guns on both sides of the divide.

'Fine with us,' bawled Staff Sergeant Morris. 'No firing for Christmas. You have my word.'

The carols had lit a flame that warmed the hearts of all. Distrust melted in the glow like butter on the hob. More songs were sung: 'Keep the Home Fires Burning' on one side, 'O Tannenbaum' on the other; a mouth organ solo from a German, a bagpipe lament from a Scot, standing upon the bank in kilt and sporran.

Goodness knows what Jerry made of that. But Jock got the biggest cheer of the night, from both sets of trenches.

At midnight, German rifles started firing. For a moment, the British thought the beastly Hun had broken his word. When they realized it was a salvo into the air to greet Christmas Day, they sent up Very lights, crackling like fireworks in the night sky.

A hundred yards apart, men waved torches and cheered:

'Happy Christmas.'

'And to you, Jack.'

'And you, Harry.'

22

Christmas Day dawned crisp and clear.

Jack woke up with a start. The Ghost of Christmas Past had flown him to the parlour of his Pompey home. Mum, Dad, and the whole tribe were sitting round the fire, unwrapping presents from the Christmas tree, wearing paper hats and pulling crackers.

Was it an exploding cracker that had woken him up? No, it was Sarge's command: 'ACTION STATIONS!'

His dream shot away, Jack was back, cold and scared, at the edge of No Man's Land.

Staff Sergeant Morris cocked his rifle and shouted out, 'Watch out! Jerry's on the move. Take aim. Fire when I say.'

A hundred men trained their sights on a single figure in a greeny-grey uniform and postman's hat. He was moving slowly across the divide, dragging something along.

A bomb? Minnie Werfer?

'Bless my cotton socks,' cried Sarge, grinning with relief. 'Blow me if he isn't planting a Christmas tree. Right in the middle of No Man's Land. Daft a'porth!'

The German had dug a hole with his bare hands and was sticking in a fir tree; its topmost branches brushed his chest. Then, standing to attention and saluting the tree, he smartly turned about and marched back the way he'd come.

'He's a brave lad,' said 'Taff' Morris. 'I could have blown him to Kingdom Come.'

'Daft as a brush,' said Harry. 'You wouldn't catch one of our lads playing silly buggers.'

111

Just then a khaki figure stood up.

'Get down, you twerp, before they blow your head off.'

'Must be shell shocked.'

A chorus of voices urged him down.

But the man stood still and calm, as if settling himself before a penalty.

'What's that in his mitts, a Christmas pudding?' cried Harry.

The men stared in alarm as the soldier took a run and kicked the 'pudding' high into the air. It bounced twice, high and fast on the crusty soil, before plopping— Splosh!—right into an icy puddle.

'How about a football match?' the kicker yelled to his mates.

'Right, you're on, chum,' shouted Jack. 'Come on, lads, we invented the game. Let's show Jerry how to play it.'

Harry, Jack, and a dozen others followed Archie, the ball's owner, into No Man's Land.

'Now, where's that darn ball?'

'Over there.'

'Nah, 'ee's in the drink. I seed 'im splash.'

At last, a joyful shout went up: 'Got 'im. Come on, me hearties, up and at 'em!'

At first, the Germans stood up and stared.

'Crazy English!'

'*Dummkopf!*'

Yet before a game could start, a bunch of shirt-sleeved Germans came scrabbling over the top. One red-faced fellow with ginger hair was shouting out, 'Hey, Tommy, what about a game. You and us, *ja*? Germany and England.'

Archie turned to his mates.

'What about it, lads?'

Nods and grins greeted the cry.

'You're on, Ginge,' Archie shouted back.

112

Cheers and shouts on both sides welcomed the match. One wisecrack bawled out:

'Why don't we play to decide the war? Then we can all go home.'

'Aye,' added another, 'and have a game each year to decide European champions. It'd save a lot of lives.'

Staff Sergeant Morris's foghorn cut through the banter.

'Stop! I give the orders round here.'

They thought he was about to halt the fun and games. But 'Taff' Morris had other things in mind.

'Let's clear the pitch first, bury the dead.'

It was only right and proper.

The Germans carried their dead comrades off. The British did the same. It wasn't a pleasant task. But you can't have a game of football with corpses cluttering up the pitch.

Men then set to clearing the barbed wire and empty shells from the strip of land. When, finally, a large enough space was free of debris, they chose captains and picked sides.

Since it was Archie's ball, they let him be England captain. Fair enough. No one minded. Herr Ginger was their *Kapitän*.

Eleven a side. Grey-green shirts versus khaki-brown shirts. All wore trousers and boots. Jackets and helmets marked the goals. There were no white lines, no referee, no whistle, no set time.

'First to five goals?' suggested Archie—ball owner, captain, and centre forward.

Grey-green shirts agreed. First a snapshot, then the game.

Red cheeks puffed out like rosy apples. Beads of sweat trickled down shiny necks. Steam curled up from backs into the crisp morning air.

It was mostly kick and rush, with a tangle of four or

113

five bodies charging after the leather ball. Despite the rough and tumble, there was never a cleaner game. If someone got knocked down, his opponent stopped to help him up. 'Sorry, mate.' 'Excuse me, comrade.'

Above the grunts and cries of players rose two sets of chants from watching fans:

'ENG-LAND! ENG-LAND! ENG-LAND!'

'DEUTSCH-LAND! DEUTSCH-LAND! DEUTSCH-LAND!'

Players responded as best they could in the mushy snow. The ball kept stopping dead as men slithered past, or squirted into water holes. The men slipped and slid all over the place. Germany's captain had to haul Archie out of a shell hole, dripping wet.

Soon you couldn't tell friend from foe as green and khaki turned to muddy brown.

All the fear and horror of war melted away in Christmas fun.

As Harry said to Jack, 'It's a damn sight better than killing each other, ain't it?'

When Germany went 4–2 up, the grey-green ranks tossed their caps into the air and cheered as if they'd won the war. Yet next time he was in front of goal, the German captain did a strange thing. Instead of shooting, he picked up the ball and went over to Archie.

'It's Christmas,' he said. 'Who cares who wins? Let's mix up the teams and let everyone join in. What do you say?'

Archie readily agreed.

'Good idea,' he said. 'Winning isn't everything. Muddyboots play Dirty Dogs.'

Both captains waved their arms towards the lines, summoning up reserves. The long and the short and the tall. Even limpers and bandaged-headers. As grey-brown men crowded round the Christmas tree, the two captains picked their teams.

'After you, Ginge,' said Archie. 'You take first pick.'

Two from one side, then two from the other—so that both teams had roughly equal numbers of English and Germans. Jack and Harry played on different sides: forty-one Muddyboots against forty-two Dirty Dogs.

Maybe that was the final score—41–42—though no one kept count.

After an hour or so, the ball landed smack-bang on a German spiked helmet marking the goal: POOOOFF! All the air hissed out.

By that time the men had had enough. Tired and happy, steaming like boiling kettles, they shook hands all round and beamed all over their muddy faces.

As they were trooping off the pitch, Archie gave a shout, 'Three cheers for Jerry. Hip-Hip Hooray! Hip-Hip Hooray! Hip-Hip Hooray!'

Herr Ginger followed suit. And German cheers followed the English from the field.

Soon soldiers were returning to the field of play, exchanging presents: cigs for chocolate, sausage for bully beef, cake for a knitted woolly hat.

Jack got pally with Fritz the Captain, and chatty with his team's goalie.

The goalie fished out a brown packet from his back pocket. With a shy smile, he showed Jack a creased photograph.

'Meine Frau und Kinder,' he said.

Jack could see what he meant. A stocky woman with long fair plaits smiled nervously out of the brown photo; two serious-looking kids were tugging at her skirts from either side.

'That's nice,' said Jack. 'Hold on, I've a snapshot of my folks . . . That's Mum and Dad, that's Florence and Dorothy my kid sisters. Floss and I are going to play for

115

Portsmouth once we've won the . . . Well, you know, when this lot's over.'

He pulled a piece of cardboard out of his pocket. Pasted on the back was Floss kicking a football. The words 'To Jack, Love Sis xxx' were written at the bottom.

'*Sehr schön*,' said the German. '*Wie heisst Du*? Name?'

'Name? Jack. Jack Loveless. And you? Name?'

'Erich, Erich Pohl.'

They gave each other a broad grin and shook hands warmly.

Just then a sudden flurry of freezing snow brought the post-match party to an end.

'Thanks, Erich. See you again, eh?'

'*Ja*, Happy Christmas, Jack.'

Soldiers were hurrying back to the trenches, waving goodbye.

23

I have grown past hate and bitterness,
I see the world as one;
Yet, though I can no longer hate,
My son is still my son.
from 'Nationality' by Mary Gilmore

Brass hats on both sides took a dim view of the truce. Even dimmer of the football match.

'Bad for morale!'

When British officers got back from Christmas lunch, the men were in mellow mood. They seemed not to hear their officer's command. Major Pattison walked down the line to restore order personally; he could not leave it to his NCOs.

To his amazement he was met by silent head-shaking, sullen grunts, and turned backs. He halted before Jack, recognizing the bearer of Freddie's bag.

'Ah, the delivery boy.'

'Yes?'

'You love your King, private.'

'Yes?'

'You've fought the Hun.'

'Yes?'

The officer lost his temper.

'You say "sir" when you address an officer! And when I say "Fire!" you fire! Got it?'

An awful hush descended. All along the trench, soldiers looked on glumly. What would happen? They thanked their lucky stars it wasn't their head on the block;

all the same they begged Jack silently *not* to grovel, *not* to cave in, *not* to squeak a measly 'Yes, sir. Sorry, sir.'

Finally, Jack sighed, looked up and stared Major Pattison in the eye . . .

'I don't want to shoot any more . . . sir.'

The tone was not defiant. It was mild but firm, like a cricket umpire giving 'Not Out'.

The major went red in the face: no one had disobeyed him before, not since prep school when he'd had to give a junior six of the best with a wet towel. That's what this blighter deserved!

Turning to the nearest soldier, he tried to restore his authority. But, emboldened by Jack's example, Harry told him straight, 'You can tell your High Command to chuck it. I've no quarrel with Fritz.'

A low muttering ran through the trench. It steadily grew like a snowball rolling downhill until it overwhelmed the officer in an avalanche of defiance.

Nervously, Major Pattison wired Company HQ.

'The men won't obey orders. They don't want to go on. They say they've had enough of killing. They want to go home.'

Right away a posse of top brass came hot foot to the Front; they were accompanied by military police and a platoon of Irish Guards.

No more talk.

They took away Archie's punctured football and held an inquiry among the NCOs.

Someone was to blame.

Somebody had to pay.

The men had to be taught a lesson.

'Frat-ern-iz-ation' was the most vile—and dangerous—of crimes. Before the assembled ranks, Staff Sergeant Morris was stripped of his three stripes. He stood, unblinking, as a colonel tore them from each arm.

'Take the prisoner under guard to Company Headquarters!'

At the colonel's command, six military policemen lined up at front, flank, and rear, then marched him off: 'Left-right, left-right, left-right.'

Taff Morris was never seen again.

Somewhere, out of sight, he was tried for 'dishonourable conduct' and 'encouraging fraternization'.

He was shot.

On the other side of the football pitch, German officers were just as resolute. Fighting spirit had to be restored double quick.

'We'll launch an attack on Boxing Day. Cold steel and iron bullets will set things right!'

'War must go on,' said the British generals.

'War must go on,' said the German generals.

And so it did. So it did.

24

'I am the enemy you killed, my friend.
I knew you in this dark; for so you frowned
Yesterday through me as you jabbed and killed.
I parried; but my hands were loath and cold.
Let us sleep now . . . '

from 'Strange Meeting' by Wilfred Owen

At dawn on Boxing Day, nineteen hundred and fourteen, the German generals kept their word. A cock crowed on a farm nearby, signalling the start.

The big guns boomed.

The bullets whizzed.

The shells showered down.

Soon the clank of steel on steel resounded on the green. With dirt spouting all about, Jack dashed down the wing, his bayonet in his hand. He'd seen Harry fall, an untidy row of red holes tearing his jacket front.

Harry didn't say a word, just dropped slowly to the ground.

Jack hurried on, firing blindly at shadows ahead, jabbing at passing shapes, wishing he were home.

All at once, a flash exploded before his face and he stumbled once, twice, falling senseless, down, down into some dark pit.

When he came to, the battle had passed on, the war had come and gone. The pitch was oddly silent, as if the players had all gone home.

Yet all at once he heard a voice. It was calling his name, 'Jack. Jack.'

Through a red-stained mist, he peered about. Dimly he made out another soldier in the shell-hole.

'*Wasser*. Water, Jack.'

Jesus Christ! It was Fritz, the German captain.

With one good hand, Jack uncorked his water bottle and put it to Fritz's lips. His eyes closed as he gulped the water down, trying to put out the fire in his torn chest.

'Thanks, Jack,' he murmured through his pain.

They were his last words.

'That's OK, mate.'

The light of day crumbled away to darkness.

25

I know the truth—forget all other truths!
No need for people anywhere on earth to fight.
Look—it's evening; look, it's nearly night:
What do you talk of—poets, lovers, generals?

The wind is calmer now, the earth is wet with dew,
The storm of stars in the sky will grow still.
And soon all of us will sleep beneath the earth, we
Who never let each other sleep above it.

'The Truth' by Marina Tsvetayeva,
trans. James Riordan

The two children left the grandfathers to themselves.

The old men talked and pointed, sighed and frowned a lot, then sat together silently, holding each other's gnarled hand. Remembering.

Meanwhile, the girl and boy walked slowly up and down the rows of headstones, reading off the names. She put right his stumbling German. When they'd squeezed through the dividing hedge, he corrected her English.

It was like school, only better, having a friend as teacher.

'What's your favourite subject?' Gretel asked.

'Sport. What's yours?'

'History.'

'Horrible History.'

He meant the dead all round them.

'Yes, it *can* be,' she said unsurely.

'You just have to count the graves. Hundreds upon hundreds upon hundreds. What a waste.'

She was silent.

'I know, let's play a game,' he said brightly. 'You stand here by an English grave. I'll be over there, by a German. We'll each shout out a name.'

She smiled.

'I've a better idea. Read out the name and say "*Nie Wieder*" as loudly as you can.'

'What does that mean?'

'Never again.'

'But we must include all the war dead,' he said.

'Yes, and if we do that, the deaths will not be wasted.'

'That's if we really mean it,' he said.

She squeezed his hand.

'NEVER AGAIN!'

'*NIE WIEDER!*'

The cries echoed across the two fields.

Crows flew up cawing.

The old soldiers looked up . . . and smiled for the first time that day.

Notes and Acknowledgements

John McCrae, 'In Flanders Fields', died after the second battle of Ypres in January 1918.

E. Bogle: lyrics from 'The Green Fields of France' (PLD Music Ltd.), reprinted by permission of Robert Brown Associates.

T. P. Cameron-Wilson, 'The Bravery of Man', was a schoolmaster before enlisting in the Grenadier Guards in August 1914. He was killed in action by the River Somme in March 1918.

Rudyard Kipling: lines from 'If', lines from 'Tommy', and 'Common Form' from 'Epitaphs of the War' all reprinted from *Rudyard Kipling's Verse: The Definitive Edition* (Hodder & Stoughton 1945), by permission of A. P. Watt Ltd on behalf of The National Trust for Places of Historic Interest or Natural Beauty. His only son John, for whom 'If' was written, was killed in September 1915.

Wilfred Owen, 'Dulce et Decorum est', 'Last Words', and 'Strange Meeting', was killed on 4 November 1918.

Saki (pen-name of H. H. Munro, 1870–1916), 'While Shepherds Watched', was a journalist and short story writer before enlisting as a trooper (he refused to become an officer) in 1914. He was killed two years later at Beaumont-Hamel in France.

Mary Gilmore: lines from 'Nationality' reprinted from *Selected Poems* (ETT Imprint, Sydney, 2000), by permission of the publisher.

Marina Tsvetayeva (1892–1941), 'The Truth', a Russian poet who lived through World War I in Russia and married a White Guard officer in the Civil War that followed World War I. She lived abroad before returning home with him and her two children in 1939. He was executed by the Soviet regime, her daughter was arrested, her son was killed in World War II, and her poetry was banned. She hanged herself in 1941.

Other books by James Riordan

Sweet Clarinet
ISBN 0 19 271795 2

I would gladly have welcomed death with a passion—as long as it stopped the pain. 'Oh, God, let me die, please, please, let me die. I'll say my prayers every night, honest, if only you let me die.'

Billy thought growing up in wartime was fun: the fiery skies, exploding factories, the noise of the blitz, playing among the rubble of the bombed houses. But then a bomb fell directly on the shelter where Billy and his mother had gone to escape the bombardment and changed Billy's life for ever.

Billy wakes up in hospital, horribly burned and longing for death—angry at a world in which he will always be a freak, an object of horror or pity, an outcast—until a precious gift from a soldier who is also disfigured gives him hope and a reason for living.

Winner of the 1999 NASEN Award and shortlisted for the Whitbread Children's Book Award

'It's a story of pain as well as triumph . . . '
Yorkshire Post

'It is very well written and impossible to put down. An amazing read!'
Shelf Life

The Prisoner
ISBN 0 19 271812 6

The bomber was tumbling through the sky like a trailing comet, belching smoke and flame. In the clear night air you could sense the pilot frantically trying to right his stricken plane. But there was nothing he could do to save himself or his tail gunner.

Tom and Iris watch the enemy aircraft coming down towards the trees and make up their minds to go hunting for souvenirs. But they find more than they had bargained for: the injured pilot, tangled in the tree by his parachute. And then the air-raid warnings sound and they all have to take shelter. While the two English children and the teenage German pilot are confined together, with the bombs falling around them, Tom and Iris listen to Martin's story. They come to realize that the real casualties of war are not only the soldiers, sailors, and airmen, but the old, the sick, the women, and the children— and that bombs don't care what side you are on.

'This powerful and moving story illustrates perfectly the conflicting emotions of wartime . . . '

Children's Book News

'An exciting story . . . '

Times Educational Supplement

War Song
ISBN 0 19 271854 1

*Nurse Cavell made no sound as the two parties of eight riflemen were
marched forward to a line six paces from the execution posts. At a
sharp command from the officer, they raised the rifles to their
shoulders. Almost at once came a second command: FIRE! So died one
of England's noblest heroines.*

Inspired by the sacrifice of Nurse Cavell, Florence and Dorothy
decide to 'do their bit', to prove that women can make a
valuable contribution to the war effort. They start work at the
munitions factory to help make the armaments desperately
needed by the soldiers at the Front—including their brother,
Jack, who was one of the first to enlist in 1914.

What Floss really wants to do, though, is be a nurse. To help
the wounded and dying, not to make the shells which cause
their injuries. But even if Floss manages to persuade the
Voluntary Aid Detachment to take her on, will she be able to
cope with the gruesome and heart-rending sights she will have
to endure and the dangers she will have to face?